The McKenna Legacy...
A Legacy of Love

To my darling grandchildren,

I leave you my love and more. Within thirty-three days of your thirty-third birthday—enough time to know what you are about—you will have in your grasp a legacy of which your dreams are made. Dreams are not always tangible things, but more often are born in the heart. Act selflessly in another's behalf, and my legacy will be yours.

> Your loving grandmother,
> Moira McKenna

P.S. Use any other inheritance from me wisely and only for good, lest you destroy yourself or those you love.

Dear Reader,

Welcome back to The McKenna Legacy and a very special book—my 25th Intrigue novel. The McKennas have a special place in my heart, and so I was thrilled by the overwhelming reader response to the first three stories, which gave me the opportunity to revisit some of my favorite characters ever.

Now I have a new favorite. Donovan Wilde may not carry the McKenna name, but he's the embodiment of their spirit. He's difficult and enigmatic, honorable and dedicated—the kind of man who demands a woman who is up for a special challenge.

And so, with pleasure, I give you Donovan and Laurel in *Never Cry Wolf*. Let me know what you think about their story and about all the McKennas by writing to me at P.O. Box 578297, Chicago, IL 60657-8297.

Patricia Rosemoor

Never Cry Wolf
Patricia Rosemoor

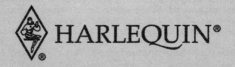

TORONTO • NEW YORK • LONDON
AMSTERDAM • PARIS • SYDNEY • HAMBURG
STOCKHOLM • ATHENS • TOKYO • MILAN • MADRID
PRAGUE • WARSAW • BUDAPEST • AUCKLAND

Thanks to the Treehaven Nature Center, University of
Wisconsin at Steven's Point, and to the volunteers of
TWIN—Timberwolf Information Network—for hosting
the educational workshop on wolf recovery where I
learned much of what I've included in this story. Any
mistakes are mine.

ISBN 0-373-22483-4

NEVER CRY WOLF

McKENNA FAMILY TREE

Descendants of MOIRA KELLY McKENNA

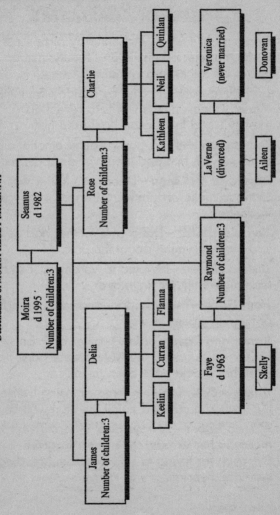

CAST OF CHARACTERS

Donovan Wilde—A McKenna by birth if not by name, he rejected his natural family until an attack leaves his father in a coma.

Laurel Newkirk—Fooled by a man who called himself Donovan, she wants to reveal his identity...and the reason he'd used her.

The Imposter—He'd gotten Laurel emotionally involved with him and then had disappeared.

Raymond McKenna—Donovan's father was trying to make certain his estranged son wasn't in danger.

Veronica Wilde—Donovan's mother had never told him everything about the past.

Joshua Harley—Devoted to Veronica, Josh can't hide his enmity for Raymond.

Ham Gault—The newspaperman was an advocate of hunting—deer or wolf.

Karen and David Tobin—Mother and son would have a lot to gain if the wolves were gone from land that should have been theirs.

Andrew Deterline—Angered at losing livestock, the farmer threatened to kill the next wolf he saw.

Magda Huber—Always odd, a hermit who kept mostly to her woods, she's never forgiven Donovan for trying to stop her from breeding wolf-dog hybrids.

If you talk to the animals
they will talk to you and you will know them.
If you do not talk to them
you will not know them
and what you do not know you will fear.
What one fears, one destroys.
                              —Chief Dan George

Prologue

1973

Moonlight scattered shadows across the narrow path as he thrashed his way through the ice-encrusted woods, but he was heedless of threat, knowing only that he had to get away. *Had* to. He wouldn't go anywhere with Raymond McKenna again, wouldn't call the man "Father," no matter what Mom said. He would hide from them both until the imposter returned alone to Chicago, as he always did—to his *real* kids—hopefully for good this time.

He ran until his narrow chest burned.

Until sweat slicked his skin beneath the parka.

Until his legs pumped his boots right through the crust, landing him in nearly two feet of snow.

Sides heaving, he lay on his side and gasped for breath, then tried to get his bearings. Eyes wide, he gazed at the surrounding territory, foreign and forbidding. Skeletal trees loomed overhead, ice-cloaked limbs outstretched like bony arms waiting to entrap him. Masked between the trees, the hard-packed path he'd been following rose and dipped, twisted and turned, before disappearing altogether.

He'd managed to run right off it.

Aa-wooo…

The ghostly sound came out of nowhere—and everywhere—spurring him to get up. The cloying white powder devoured his legs with each step, only allowing him inches instead of feet. Should have taken his snowshoes, but then he wouldn't have been able to go so fast.

How far?

He didn't recognize a thing, had never actually been alone in the woods before. Mom was gonna kill him. *If* she found him. He swallowed hard. How many miles from the road? Might as well be a zillion as a couple.

His chest squeezed tighter.

He was lost.…

Not that he wanted to go back. Not with *him* there. He wasn't afraid, definitely not afraid. Only…he was starting to get cold. His teeth began to chatter and his skin pebbled against his damp clothes. Snow still enveloped his legs, and now a burst of wind slapped at his bare face.

What to do?

Find shelter.…

Instinct drove him farther from the path, slowly, torturously, his goal a fallen, burned tree, a victim of lightning. The woods were closing in on him. Whispers creeping along his spine. The forest talking to him. Chiding him for being so foolish.

Maybe no one would ever find him.

Maybe he'd freeze to death.

That would show them!

A lump lodged in his throat as he reached for a stump and pulled himself free of the drift and onto a solid incline between two fat pines. Fumbling in his jacket pocket with a mittened hand, he found his Swiss Army knife and, awkwardly freeing the blade, began stripping branches. The fragrance of fresh pine soothed him as he covered the ground next to the log that was split and hollow at its core.

Shelter. A bed.

A strange feeling came over him and his hair ruffed, standing straight on end. A sound that might have been imagined, that seemed to come from deep inside his head, made him whip around to check behind him.

''Wh-who's there?''

From the shadowy forest slipped a menacing figure, little more than a silhouette against the luminous snow. A four-footed creature with shaggy black fur and glowing yellow eyes.

His breath caught in his throat as he stared.

A dog?

The nose was too prominent. The legs too long and thin. No dog he'd ever seen had eyes like that.

So, why wasn't he afraid? And why was that other fear—the one of being alone and lost, maybe worse—fading?

He wasn't alone anymore.

That knowledge was all that mattered. Renewed courage filling him, gaze steady on the mesmerizing yellow eyes, he hunkered down and held out his hand....

Chapter One

Moon high, Donovan Wilde loped through the thick woods, his step light, landing whisper-quiet against the newly fallen snow. Heart racing, breath laving his face in frosty billows, he followed impulse alone.

Something was wrong.

The alarm was internal...gut instinct...prescience...call it what he might.

He *knew*.

Someone alien invaded his forest. A two-footed creature. A man.

But whom?

The same someone whose tracks he'd found several times over the past weeks? Tracks he didn't recognize. Tracks that raised his suspicions like the hair on his scalp.

Aa-wooo...

The initial howl was followed by others, each a different pitch, as if the wolves were singing...harmonizing...when, in truth, they were sending coded messages to each other. To him. To anyone who cared to listen and to understand.

Donovan howled back.

Gradually, the urgency gripping him receded. The tightness in his chest relented and his muscles unfurled. His step slowing, he reconnoitered, assimilating and analyzing every nuance of his surroundings, not with the senses used by most people, but with a singular one inherited from a grandmother he'd never met. Or so the story went.

No perception of the other presence. *Gone.* His forest was safe once again.

But from whom? A hunter ignoring the postings? Or from some danger more sinister?

Aa-wooo…

Ar-ar-ar…

Ow-ow-wow…

Reaching the edge of a clearing, he stopped dead in his tracks and joined the chorus. Closed his eyes, raised his head and howled, then concentrated on the faint impressions rapidly gathering inside his mind.

Images wavering from side to side…a flash of trees…a glimpse of a rise…then a field of snow…

A shared vision drawing ever closer.

Flicking open his eyes and focusing them, Donovan quickly narrowed his gaze toward the other side of the clearing. A moment later, a familiar silhouette slipped out of the forest and stilled.

As did his very breath.

"OKAY, SO I SAY, 'Hi, I'm a friend of your…a *close* friend of your son's, and he up and took a powder on me.' So old Dad raises his eyebrows and says—'' she shifted into a deeper tone "'—And what do you expect me to do about it, young lady? Retrieve him for you?'"

Laurel Newkirk felt a tad better rehearsing her spiel as she vainly searched for parking on a side street. That was the problem with the fancy neighborhoods on the near north side of Chicago, especially at night. Too many vehicles, too few empty spaces. She circled the block.

"Then what?" she wondered aloud.

What if he'd meant to disappear on her?

Laurel had sensed he hadn't taken her hesitation lightly, even though he'd covered his emotions with a bright smile and an understanding nod. He would definitely have interpreted her asking for time to think about his proposal as a rejection. After all, he hadn't called since. Laurel swallowed hard. Was she nuts, or what? A handsome, charming, intelligent man, dedicated to a cause she believes in, offers her the big, loving family she's always longed for, and she has to think about it?

Oh, his proposal had been sooo tempting.

And yet...

As she turned the corner, car lights flicked on up the street. Her foot automatically slammed into the accelerator. She zoomed forward and came to a screeching halt inches from the other vehicle as it pulled away from the curb. The driver threw on the brakes and blared his horn at her. Properly chastised, she sank low in her seat and grimaced. The other driver took off; she waited until he'd turned the corner before claiming the space.

"Or what if I'm jumping the gun here, and I throw

the man into a panic for nothing?" she muttered. "Maybe I should just say, 'I've lost touch with your son and want to look him up. Do you know where I might find him?'"

But the polite inquiry sounded false, even to her own ears. If her interest was so casual, and all she'd wanted was an address, she could have called.

What if something had happened to him?

That was her real worry, the thing that had kept her up the past few nights, talking to her three dogs, seven cats and lone rabbit—foundlings, all—who'd had no choice but to listen. Just because she hadn't agreed to marry Donovan right off didn't mean she had no feelings for the man. Of course she cared about him. And fear for his safety had overcome her reluctance to seek out his father, a powerful U.S. congressman, who happened to be in town for the weekend.

"How about, 'Sir, I'm sure it's nothing,'" she mumbled as she danced along the icy sidewalk, "'but I can't seem to locate your son.'"

A hint of something possibly being wrong, but nothing too extreme. Yep, that was the ticket.

Still, she stood before the brick row house—where inviting golden light spilled from the first-floor windows—and shifted from one foot to the other while working up her nerve. No doubt, her initial instinct had been correct, and the rejection thing had driven Donovan away. While on the surface he'd appeared to be polished and together, underneath was a more complex story.

She knew all about facades.

From the first, she'd sensed Donovan was deeply

troubled...maybe the very reason she'd been drawn to him...certainly the reason she hadn't been able to commit herself. Always having to be the strong one made her long for a man with an even broader pair of shoulders. A guilty feeling at being too harsh edged her assessment of Donovan's not quite fitting the bill. Yet, undoubtedly he'd gone back to his woods seeking solace. Her stomach coiled into a knot. She was probably going to look pretty foolish if she went through with this.

But appearing foolish came a poor second to abandoning someone in trouble, Laurel told herself with a sigh. And after all she'd been through, surviving a little humiliation would be a piece of cake.

Fixing her gaze on the high first-floor entrance door flanked by stern-looking stone lions, Laurel knew she'd just talked herself out of choices.

"JAMES MUST BE busting his buttons now that your time is so near," Raymond McKenna told his niece, unable to keep the gruffness from his tone even when he tried. "That brother o' mine always had to be first, no matter if he's fathering or grandfathering a bairn."

Enveloped from behind in her husband Tyler's arms, Keelin smiled, her freckled face full and radiant as it had been during these last months of her pregnancy. She was due within the week, the reason Raymond had gathered the family together upon his return from D.C., so they could all celebrate the imminent birth of the first McKenna grandchild...even if its *legal* last name would be Leighton.

"Aye, Da does relish having the upper hand."

Keelin winked. "But there's no shame in going him one better."

Raymond laughed and glanced over at his daughter-in-law Rosalind, even bigger, if more than a month from her delivery date. "Two better." He clucked to himself. "Another set of McKenna triplets."

"Gran is surely pleased with herself at the mischief she wrought."

"What's that about our dear Moira?" Skelly asked, entering the parlor from the kitchen and heading straight for his wife. "I always miss everything."

Eyeing the size of his daughter-in-law's belly, Raymond said dryly, "Not *everything*, boyo." Before he could go on, the bell jarred him. He frowned, immediately irritated at the thought of the pleasant evening with his family being interrupted. "Now, who could that be?"

Trailing behind her brother, Aileen asked, "Want me to get it, Dad?"

"You've done more than enough getting the dinner together, sweetheart."

The bell sounded again, and Raymond stormed toward the front door, ready to chew off the intruder's head. Who in the world dared disturb his first Friday night off in ages? He was in a fine temper when he threw open the door.

"What is it?"

The woman on the other side took a startled step back. Her mouth opened but nothing came out. She stared at him, wide-eyed and dumbstruck.

"Will you be wasting my time then, woman?"

"I, uh...uh, you're Congressman Raymond Mc-

Kenna, right? I need to talk to you about something important.''

He couldn't believe the chit was seeking a political favor tonight of all nights. "Out with it!"

She stared at him a moment more, as if she didn't know what to make of him.

Or he of her, Raymond thought, eyeing her disheveled appearance.

"I'm looking for your son. He and I...well, we...um, he disappeared and I'm trying to find him," she said in a rush, after which she let out a long breath.

He started. What had Skelly gotten himself into? He had a wife, the glorious woman who was bearing his child—three of them—and he'd had something to do with this one? What could that son of his have been thinking?

"Skelly," he called in a deceptively calm tone, "can you be joining me for a moment?"

Not that he'd set a good example for anyone when it came to matters of the heart. But he'd hoped for better sense from his children.

Entering the foyer, Skelly asked, "What's up?"

"Keep your voice down, boyo. Find out what your chit wants and be rid of her."

He ignored the young woman's shocked expression. What had she hoped for? An open-armed welcome?

"My what?" Sounding puzzled, Skelly glanced out the door. "What's going on here?"

"You tell me," she responded. "Who are you?"

"The man you came to find!" an exasperated Raymond nearly yelled as he felt the veins in his neck and forehead bulge. "My son!"

"Ah-h, you must be Skelly McKenna, the older brother," the woman said, sounding appeased. "I'm Laurel Newkirk." She switched her attention back to him. "You don't understand, Mr....uh, Congressman McKenna. I didn't mean him. I'm looking for your other son. Donovan. I thought maybe you could tell me where to find him."

Raymond took a better look at her.

Long brown hair tangled around a set of ridiculous-looking earmuffs. Long legs encased in slim jeans, feet in hikers' boots. And in between, a slender body dwarfed in an olive drab military-type jacket with half a dozen bulging pockets.

This was starting to make sense.

Calming himself, he asked, "You drove all the way from northern Wisconsin to ask *me* where to find that scoundrel?"

"Then he's not here. In Chicago, I mean."

"He wouldn't step foot in a big city unless he was hog-tied and forced," Skelly muttered.

"You're wrong," she countered, a frown puzzling her forehead. "Your brother *has* been here. Quite a lot over the past few months, as a matter of fact. But a little more than a week ago, he up and disappeared without so much as a goodbye."

Raymond could see the lass was truly worried. He stepped back, even knowing his pleasant evening was about to come to an abrupt end. Donovan always had had a way of spoiling things for everyone.

Swinging the door open wide, he grumbled, "You'd better come in, then."

NOT EXACTLY the reception she'd been looking for.

Thinking of Donovan, Laurel swallowed her renewed reluctance and entered the stately old home with its twelve-foot ceilings, parquet-floored foyer and handworked wood. She stuffed her earmuffs and gloves in a pocket, then followed Skelly into the living room where several more sets of eyes immediately focused on her.

Laurel stopped dead in her tracks. "Oh, no, I'm interrupting a party...."

"Family dinner," Skelly amended, then gave her a mocking smile. "But don't worry about it. We could use a little excitement. Life has been too tame lately. This is Laurel Newkirk," he told the others. "Have a seat, please."

Laurel took the chair he indicated, but she couldn't help feeling a bit intimidated as her gaze swept the flawlessly appointed room with its antiques and obviously real artwork. Her own furniture was merely old, if well-polished—what else should she have with so many animals?—the art on her walls nicely framed wildlife and nature posters, reflecting her interests. Two different worlds, as far apart as she was from the other females present.

The fair-haired woman wearing exotic jewelry and a loosely constructed jacket in jewel tones must be Aileen. Donovan had told her his younger sister was a healer, a massage therapist, and as unconventional as they came. The one with dark red curly hair and freckles in a flowing yellow silk dress she recognized as his cousin Keelin, an herbalist whose gift—and curse—was the ability to dream through another's eyes. And, of course, the classic blonde wearing a soft blue maternity suit had to be Skelly's wife Rosalind Van Straaten, heiress and chic businesswoman who'd masterminded the wildly successful Temptress Day Spas.

That the whole family was present seemed like a sign. Surely one of them would be able to relieve her mind.

"According to our guest, Donovan's missing," Skelly was telling them all.

"How would anyone know?" Rosalind asked with a laugh.

Focusing her attention back to the purpose at hand, Laurel frowned at the other woman. "What does that mean?"

"It's not like any of us has seen him for years," Skelly explained as he sat next to his wife and wrapped an arm around her shoulders. "Roz has never even met my errant brother."

"Nor have I," put in Keelin's husband.

Errant? Years? "But he's been in Chicago..."

"When?" Aileen demanded, sounding hurt. "Where?"

Confused, Laurel stared at her. Donovan had told her his family was close-knit. If so, why did she seem to know more about his doings than they did?

Arms crossed over his chest, Raymond stood guard over his family when he said, "So, you met him here."

"No. In Wisconsin." Nerves slid her hands over the brocade chair arms. "At an ecology workshop about timber wolves."

"He actually gave a workshop?" Aileen asked, hurt turning to amazement. "To other *people?*"

"Well, no...I mean he wasn't giving the workshop, but that doesn't matter." This wasn't going at all as she'd imagined. She felt their doubt...as great as her own. Mouth dry as cotton, fingers digging into the chair arms, she continued. "What does matter is that we became...friends."

"In Wisconsin," Skelly said.

"No, here."

"You're telling us my son is living in Chicago?"

She shook her head as much to deny the suspicion gripping her as to answer. "He had his work in Wisconsin, but he visited when he could. Actually, it became quite a bit." The details were awkward and not something she wanted to share. Especially not now when she felt as though she were the center of an inquisition. Finding a loose thread in the brocade, she fingered it. "Then, a little more than a week ago, we had a slight disagreement and he disappeared."

"A lover's spat?" Aileen asked.

Lies, Laurel thought. Donovan had lied to her about his relationship with his family. But why?

"He asked me to marry him and I...didn't say yes."

"So the boyo up and disappeared again!"

"That's Donovan." Aileen shook her head. "I just can't believe he'd be sociable enough to come out of his woods for a woman in the first place. No offense."

"None taken." But she was offended, if not at that exact comment. "And he's very sociable."

"Donovan? Sociable?"

Laurel knew she was being defensive when she insisted, "He's charming. And funny. And sweet."

"You *are* talking about Donovan *Wilde*, right?" Skelly asked. "The loner who's...plainspoken."

His nice way of saying rude? Laurel wondered. Reality was spinning away, further and further from her grasp. She lunged out of the chair and felt something give. Her fingers were still gripping the loose thread. Appalled, she stared down at a seam beginning to split open, then quickly moved away from the chair before she could do more damage.

"I don't understand." She could barely make her throat work, barely get out the words. "You make him sound like a complete stranger...and after everything he's told me about all of you." She glared at the McKennas who gave each other wide-eyed looks.

"He doesn't even know us anymore," Skelly insisted. "Never wanted to in the first place. Not even when we were kids."

Were they talking about the same Donovan?

Hovering near a table loaded with framed photographs, she searched for the Donovan she knew. When she couldn't immediately place him, a sick feeling filled her. A hand reached past her, picked up one that had been relegated to the rear.

"This is my younger son."

A photograph taken nearly twenty years before, Laurel noted, undoubtedly a high school shot. How odd that his own father didn't have anything more recent. And how deeply estranged they must be, she thought, staring at the boy in the picture. He was wiry, had dark hair and pale eyes that closed him off from the photographer.

He *could* be her Donovan. Had to be.

Nodding, she said, "Yes, that's…" But in truth couldn't finish. "I think."

"I'm not liking this," Raymond said.

Neither was she.

"I'm going to call his mother." Stalking out of the room, Raymond said, "Don't leave."

Not that her legs would even support her if she wanted to go. She clung to the table's edge.

Why would Donovan have lied to her? Or had he? He'd told her about the various members of his family, about how they'd come to each other's rescue when one of them had been in trouble…but had he actually painted himself in the picture? She'd thought so…but now she wasn't certain.

"Question," Aileen said. "How can you be so close to my brother and not know how to find him?"

"His job takes him all over northern Wisconsin…wherever the wolves are. Wolves don't have addresses or phone numbers. He always contacted me."

And she'd assumed that he'd stayed with his family while in the city…at least the first several weeks that they'd seen each other. But she'd been wrong. Now she knew he wouldn't have been welcome with any of them.

What if he'd spent his whole life on the outside looking in? Raymond McKenna had three children, each of whom had a different mother, Donovan's being the only one he hadn't actually married. From the first, she'd sensed Donovan was troubled behind the quick smile and devil-may-care attitude. Maybe this was why—his being a stranger to his own family.

Laurel's mind spun, searching for some plausible explanation for the lies.

They didn't know him at all. Not like she did. They didn't want to. And he'd never wanted to admit it. That *had* to be it. He'd wanted her to believe that he was part of a big, close-knit family because that's what he'd wanted for himself.

Or was it because he'd known that's what *she'd* wanted for *herself?*

At the moment, Laurel wanted to flee from this house, from the people who had excluded a member of their own family because he wasn't really "one of them." But more, she wanted to know that Donovan was all right, so she waited until Raymond returned.

His expression didn't reassure her.

"Veronica hasn't seen him, not for weeks. Not that that's unusual. He doesn't go into town unless he needs supplies."

"Town?" Laurel echoed. "As in, one particular town?"

"Iron Lake. His mother owns the café there. He moved back to be near her when he left Idaho. I know he can't get utilities living in that shack in the middle of nowhere, but you'd think he could afford a cell phone!"

A shack, perhaps, but a place Donovan called home...*more lies.* Laurel was past stunned. She was speechless.

"Something is amiss," Keelin said.

Tyler asked, "One of your visions?"

"No need to see this...'tis the legacy and she's the proof." Her haunted eyes were fixed on Laurel.

The room went still and Laurel's flesh crawled. She knew nothing about any legacy...but obviously everyone else in the room did.

Skelly broke the silence. "Donovan *is* the next in line."

"We're bound to be repeating it," Keelin whispered, voice trembling, "over and over till one of us doesn't survive."

Tyler knelt before his wife and took her hands. "Don't get yourself all worked up, sweetheart. Remember the baby." He gently touched her stomach.

"Aye, the bairn."

But Laurel could tell Keelin couldn't swallow her upset so easily, and she didn't think it was the pregnancy alone that was making the other woman so emotional.

"First Keelin, then Skelly and Kathleen, now Donovan," Aileen said brightly, as if this family legacy were a positive thing. "You all know what that means. He's about to commit himself to the love of his life."

Again, every set of eyes in the room turned toward Laurel. She shifted uneasily. Donovan *had* committed himself...

The weight on her shoulders grew.

Keelin insisted, "He needs warning."

And no one argued.

"I'm going to find him and do just that," Raymond said grimly. "Now." He was already heading for the foyer.

"Dad, you can't drive all the way up there alone."

He paused to glare at his daughter. "I'm not feeble yet."

Before she could consider the ramifications, Laurel assured Aileen, "And he won't have to go alone. I started this." As confused as she now was by the lies

Donovan had told her, she meant to carry through. "I can't leave it until I find him."

Raymond protested, "I don't need anyone—"

She cut him off. "Well I do," she said truthfully. "My car's a beater. And if you won't let me come with you, I'll just have to follow you and take my chances that I won't break down somewhere along the road."

Raymond stared at her, as if trying to gauge her mettle. His nod was as curt as his invitation.

"Then you'll be needing to hurry."

LAUREL'S OFFERS to take a turn driving fell on deaf ears both times they stopped for gas. And since Donovan's father didn't seem inclined to talk, there was nothing left for her to do but think. Or sleep.

Sleep grew more and more alluring....

She awoke to utter darkness—country darkness—but for the green glow of the dash. The moon seemed to have done a disappearing act. They'd left the highway behind and were wending their way along some narrow, ice-patched back road that cut through a thick stand of winter-barren trees.

"Where are we?"

"In his woods."

"Literally? Donovan owns them?"

"Lives in them like his damned wolves."

Not exactly an invitation to ask more questions. Laurel had the distinct impression that Raymond McKenna approved neither of his son nor of his son's charges. So, why was he rushing into nowhere to find Donovan in the middle of the night?

Why was *she?* What was she trying to protect Donovan from?

Venturing to find out, she asked, "What's this about some family legacy?"

"You wouldn't understand."

"Not if you don't explain."

She didn't think he would, so she concentrated on the path the car's high beam cut before them.

Twisting...turning...desolate.

When Raymond said, "My mother Moira was an unusual woman," he surprised her. "A *bean feasa* they called her before she died. You see, she had certain...gifts."

"Like Keelin's."

"Yes. Not that they helped her keep her family together. We betrayed each other when we were young and foolish—my brother, sister and I. My mother didn't want the same fate for her nine grandchildren. She left them a legacy of the heart...but one that went hand in hand with danger."

Even as a shudder coursed through her, Laurel said, "Surely you don't believe that."

"I've lived long enough to see many things come to pass that people don't want to believe. Keelin's the proof. And Skelly. And their cousin Kathleen, as well. My God, I almost lost one son...."

Donovan in danger. Laurel feared it could be true.

Was *that* the reason he'd seemed so troubled beneath his smiles? And the real reason he'd disappeared? How arrogant that she'd assumed *she* had been responsible.

Mesmerized by the ribbon of road ahead, she wondered what she would say to him when they came face-to-face…so absorbed in the drama of it that a sudden movement from the woods startled her into crying out.

"Watch it!"

Even as a deer bounded across the road mere feet in front of them, Raymond wrenched the wheel to the right. "Hang on!"

The car pitched, jolted, then slid, veering off the icy pavement. He slammed on the brakes. The vehicle jerked and pulsed, tipped and twisted, before finally coming to a shuddering stop.

"Are you all right?"

World cockeyed, hand pressed against the dash to steady herself, she gasped, "Yeah." And, thank heaven, so was the deer, who escaped certain death. "You?"

"I've been better."

He turned on the interior light and put a hand to his head. His fingers came away dabbled with blood.

"You *are* hurt!"

"A bump, no more," he insisted. "Not enough to stop me."

"But this ditch may be," she muttered.

Several minutes of his trying to ease the car out of the culvert proved her right. Between the pitch of the vehicle's nose and the icy snow under the wheels, they weren't going anywhere.

"Now what?" she asked when he stopped trying and cut the lights if not the engine and heater.

"We can't be far from my son's cabin." Raymond pulled a flashlight from under his seat. "I'll find it."

"I'm coming with you."

"No. Stay." He indicated the car's cell phone.

"Call for service. Tell them we're on the old paved road three miles or so north of town. I'm thinking it'll take hours for them to get here. When I find the cabin, I'll fetch you. In the meantime, you stay comfortable and warm."

"But—"

"Don't be arguing with me, woman!"

With a sense of misgiving, Laurel watched him wade into the snow and cut through the woods—until he and his thin beam of light were shortly sucked up by the surrounding dark. Dutifully, she called for help, not as simple a task as she might like, considering she couldn't pin down their exact location. But satisfied that someone would be looking for them, she told herself to relax, though it was hardly possible when she was focused on the dash with its digital clock.

Five minutes passed.

"Good move, Laurel, letting a through-and-through city person go out there alone."

The sound of her own voice soothed her....

...until five minutes stretched to ten.

"Like he knows these woods," she muttered, thinking she ought to go find him. "As if *you* do."

When nearly twenty minutes had passed, she couldn't stand it any longer.

"And him having smacked his head..."

She had to go after him.

Fetching her keys from one of her jacket pockets, she checked the miniature flashlight that hung from the ring. The beam was limited in nature, but steady. She killed the engine but left the keys in case Raymond somehow returned to the car first. Then she slipped into her earmuffs and gloves and out of the car.

The cold was shocking. Though she'd dressed sensibly enough for Chicago, northern Wisconsin was another matter, no matter that it was late March. More layers of clothing were called for. And something on her head. Her exposed face was already growing stiff. Her breath froze white on the icy air.

Ignoring the strange night sounds of the deep woods—cracking and shushing, undoubtedly both products of the wind—she set off.

The congressman's tracks were easy enough to follow. Younger and lighter, she could move faster and expected to catch up to him handily. But she hadn't gone far when his tracks first crossed then joined with another set. Assuming these were Donovan's tracks, she paused and vaguely studied the pattern made by his soles against the snow.

Donovan.

"So, I ask him, 'What could you have been thinking—up and disappearing on me like that? And what's the big idea of pretending you were so close to your family and all?'"

Right. Accusations guaranteed to put him on the defensive.

More sounds, closer this time, raised the hair at the back of her neck.

Aa-wooo...

Ar-ar-ar...

She caught her breath. Howling. *Wolves!* A thrill shot through her at the idea of actually seeing a wolf in the wild...if not under these exact circumstances. There'd never been an unprovoked attack by a healthy wolf.... She knew that from the workshop she'd taken. And yet...another howl set her off again. Though she threw a few nervous glances over her shoulder, she forced herself to maintain the same brisk pace while considering what she would say to Donovan when they came face-to-face.

"I could be a little more tactful, at least to start. 'Donovan, you had me so worried,'" she practiced saying in a softer voice. "'Surely you know I care about you.'"

Just not enough to accept a proposal.

Her musings were interrupted by a human bellow. A voice. A man's voice. She stopped to place it, still some distance ahead. Angry words were uttered low, too low for her to understand...but she thought she recognized the voice.

"Congressman McKenna?" she called. "Is that you?"

No answer.

Then she caught another sound...one barely audible but menacing. Her chest tightened.

"Congressman—"

A growl, followed by a shout, cut her short. She ran, digging her boots hard into the snowy path, placing one foot in front of the other until she reached what seemed to be a clearing. Finally slowing, she flashed her minilight around but saw no one. Her neck hair was at attention, however. All senses at high alert, she moved in, turning in a circle, challenging the surrounding darkness with her tiny beam.

This had to be the place...and yet, Raymond McKenna seemed to have disappeared.

Even as she wondered what to do next, her heel hit

something unyielding. Before she could catch herself, she went down hard. Gasping, she reached out...but her hand didn't connect with the expected tree stump.

The obstacle was soft. Clothed.

A body!

"Omigod!"

Even as she jumped back, her light caught the long overcoat.

"Congressman?"

Finding it hard to swallow, she shone the thin beam up his torso to his withered face. His eyes were closed...but his throat lay opened and bloody.

Savaged!

She clapped a hand over her mouth so she wouldn't gag. What could have done this to him? Even knowing better, *wolf* came to mind. She had heard howls.... Before she could pull herself together to check for a pulse, a footfall crunching against a crusty layer of snow startled her.

She fell back, her light beaming up to meet glittering eyes in a wild animal face....

Chapter Two

Just then, the moon slid out from beneath the cloud cover. Its silver wash clarifying the threat.

Man rather than beast loomed over her. A bizarre head covering made from a complete animal skin, possibly a coyote—paws, tail and head intact—protected him to the shoulders. Skins covered the rest of him, as well. His fringed outer garments, all the way down to his soft, knee-high moccasins, were undoubtedly constructed of deer hide. A knife was sheathed at his waist. And secured to his feet were long, narrow snowshoes.

Looking every bit the eighteenth-century trapper, the menacing stranger leaned down toward her.

Would he try to kill her, too?

Assuming he had something to do with the attack on Raymond, she crabbed away from him, the ground icy against her bottom, and marshaled her strength to fight. But the stranger ignored her as he knelt by the fallen man.

His sharp intake of breath knifed through her. And she wanted to protest as he slipped a hand beneath the congressman's coat to his chest. Searching for what? Valuables?

But his hand came away empty and he softly growled, "He's alive." Then quickly checked Raymond over for other injuries.

Relief filling her, she incautiously muttered, "No thanks to *you,* right?"

He cocked his head and glared at her in answer.

She shrank away from him again. His gaze held hers for no more than a few seconds…long enough to make her sweat inside. And to get angry with herself for being so servile, no matter how imposing the stranger seemed to her. Thankful that Donovan's father was merely hurt and unconscious, deciding to demand that the stranger *do* something, Laurel nervously licked at her lips. A mistake. The air immediately iced them over.

Through Popsicle lips, she managed to ask, "Are you going to let him bleed to death, or what?"

Ignoring her, the stranger took a moment to inspect Raymond's neck wound, after which he carefully freed the older man's scarf, filled it with snow and wrapped the impromptu cold pack against the exposed throat.

No blood had actively pumped from the wound that she could see. Did that mean whatever had savaged his throat had missed an artery? Or that the intense cold had merely slowed down the life-threatening activity?

"How bad is it?" she demanded even as he slid his hands under Raymond.

Not a word to her, as if she weren't even there.

With a grunt, he rose, limp body dangling from his arms. He started off, and Laurel hastened to her feet.

"Hey, Trapper Dan! What are you doing? Where are you taking him?"

Was he deaf, or what? Laurel wondered when he continued to slight her.

She scrambled after him, regretting her incautious first words to the stranger. Okay, so maybe she'd jumped to conclusions and he'd had nothing to do with the attack. But surely he could tell she was freaked by the situation. He *could* make allowances.

Moonlight now glinted off the snow-covered ground, the silvery blue glow illuminating the area and rendering her flashlight useless. She returned it to her pocket and concentrated on keeping up. Even burdened as he was, the stranger swiftly glided across virgin snow toward a stand of trees.

Laurel would kill for a pair of snowshoes like his. Her feet kept breaking through the top crust, sinking her to her knees in what had to be two feet of fresh powder. Determined to keep up, she was exhausting herself trying.

"Hey, wait a minute, would you?"

But Trapper Dan kept going, through the woods and down an incline until he reached a vehicle. She would have guessed his transport of choice to be a dogsled and team rather than the dark four-by-four parked on what looked to be an unpaved, uncleared logging road.

The time it took him to open the back, place Donovan's father inside and remove his snowshoes before climbing in was enough for her to catch up. Panting from the effort—sweating inside her clothes despite the bitter cold—she didn't bother to ask permission. She quickly clambered into the back where he'd already folded a blanket and was using it as a makeshift pillow to elevate Raymond's head and torso.

Silently, they faced each other over the fallen congressman.

The dome light's glow afforded her a better look at his face. Sharp featured. A little grizzled, as if he hadn't shaved for days. Expression grim and familiar somehow... Amber eyes glittering as he inspected her with equal intensity. The oddest sensation filled her...as if he were able to see beyond her eyes and climb right inside her.

Sucking in her breath, Laurel pulled back and broke the connection.

Trapper Dan removed the improvised ice bag and checked the wound. It didn't look quite as bad as she'd imagined, though as the congressman's chest slowly expanded, the area slowly pooled with blood.

Hating the fact that she felt helpless in such a serious situation, she vowed to take a first-aid class as soon as possible. In the meantime, she found Raymond's lifeless hand and squeezed.

As if good vibrations could bring him around.

Glancing down, she noticed the end of his sleeve was ragged. Ripped. As if he'd put up his hand to stop the attack.

Digging into a rawhide pouch, the stranger pulled out a battered kit. A moment later, he was placing a gauze pad over the wound. Blood seeped through. He added another pad and topped it with a piece of plastic, then taped the layers down to the skin. Again digging into the pouch, he retrieved a pair of socks.

Puzzled, Laurel couldn't help herself. "You really think he needs dry socks now?"

Not so much as hesitating to give her one of his looks, he tied the socks together, then wrapped them around the congressman's neck and secured the ends, turning them into an improvised compression bandage. From the kit he then produced a rectangular packet, which he twisted a couple of times before placing it over the bandaged area.

"Hold it there. Give it some pressure, but don't cut off his air."

A direct order she was quick to obey. Cold from the emergency pack immediately seeped through her leather glove. She watched in silence as he closed the back of the vehicle and slid behind the wheel. And as they took off, she chewed at her thawing lips.

"Hey, Trapper Dan..." Laurel saw his eyes flash to the rearview mirror. "Sorry...about before, I mean. I was a little freaked out, as I'm sure you can imagine. And then *you* popped out of nowhere dressed like some kind of wild frontiersman..."

His eyes shifted back to the road, leaving her feeling too foolish for more words.

The fast and bumpy ride that took them out of the woods stretched into forever. Snowflakes dusted the windshield and swirled around the truck even before they exited the woods. Not once did Raymond stir. Nor did she notice any signs of his revival on the long highway drive. *How long?* Were there no nearby medical facilities? Considering Trapper Dan's normal mode of response, she didn't figure there was much point in asking.

But her mind was spinning almost as fast as the wheels of their vehicle.

Had someone been arguing with the congressman or not? Could he have found his son? Had one of the wolves attacked, after which Donovan had left his own father to die?

She couldn't believe it. Not the Donovan she knew. He might be troubled and not altogether truthful with her, but she couldn't be mistaken about his innate decency. Maybe the other man had been a hunter. A trespasser who'd been scared off by the sudden attack…

Laurel sought answers where there were none. At least not until Raymond came around and could speak for himself. Their turning off the highway alerted her that their journey was coming to an end.

"Hang on, Congressman," she whispered while squeezing his hand. "We're almost there."

The Tracker careened into a lot and came to a heart-jolting stop. Trapper Dan flew out of the driver's seat, then raced across the sidewalk and through a door emblazoned with red lettering: Emergency. A moment later, two medics, a man and a woman, rushed out to the truck, a crash cart between them.

Even as Laurel opened the rear door, they waved her away from Raymond. She scooted out as they rushed in. She gasped in cold drafts of the night air mixed with snow as if she'd been oxygen deprived. Her feet seemed rooted to the pavement that was already icing over as they carefully loaded Donovan's father onto the crash cart.

Familiar. Too familiar.

Her pulse picked up. Her heart banged against her ribs. She'd almost forgotten how much she hated hospitals. But stepping inside, it came back to her in one huge, sweeping rush of memories.

The sterile atmosphere...the sense of urgency...the smell of antiseptics...

Everything happened so fast that she didn't realize Trapper Dan hadn't come back out until she saw him talking to an older, balding man in scrubs, undoubtedly the physician on duty for the night. He clapped the stranger on the shoulder and followed the crash cart into an inner room.

"You can wait here," said the admitting clerk, whose name tag identified her as Sophie. She indicated a small alcove with several chairs and a television mounted on the wall.

Taking a deep breath to steady herself, Laurel asked, "Don't you want personal information on the victim first?" Talking would help keep the memories at bay. And with her kind eyes and sympathetic smile, the woman appeared pleasant enough.

But she said, "We have what we need for right now. Don't you worry." She patted Laurel's arm. "Congressman McKenna is in good hands."

Laurel started. "How did you know who...you couldn't have seen his driver's license yet." She was certain the medics hadn't taken the time to search for a wallet and she hadn't identified him by name to anyone.

"We didn't need to see his license. Not with his son here. He said he'll take care of the paperwork once the medical staff is seeing to his father."

"His son? You mean Donovan?"

"Donovan Wilde," Sophie confirmed.

Laurel's head began to spin again. She looked around but didn't see him. "You're telling me Donovan's *here?* Where?" How could he have known?

The other woman's brow pinched. "I thought you two were together."

Following Sophie's gaze to the only other person in the room, Laurel felt her knees give way.

DONOVAN DISPASSIONATELY watched his father's companion sink into a chair, her openmouthed gape aimed at him.

The telephone rang and the admitting clerk scurried back to her station to answer it, leaving them some privacy. In tight control, he drew closer, preparing himself for a verbal barrage. This one had an unstoppable mouth on her.

So, not surprisingly, the woman immediately demanded, "Who are you *really?*"

"More to the point, who are *you?* And—"

"Laurel Newkirk," she interrupted.

"—what are you up to?" he concluded, registering the unfamiliar name.

"Up to?" Her pale blue eyes hardened into shards of ice as she leveled a penetrating gaze at him. "You're the one who should be answering that. Congressman McKenna and I were looking for his son."

"Why?"

What did the old man want with him after all these years? And why should he even care?

"What's it to you?"

"Nothing," he lied.

To cover, Donovan busied himself, removing his

outer gear as he remembered how still his father lay when he'd found him. He'd seemed so much older...more vulnerable...but Donovan knew that had to be a sham. His memory was long and vivid. He threw the headgear and deerskin jacket on one chair, then himself into another. Her expression disbelieving, Laurel didn't take her eyes off him.

He returned the favor.

She'd removed those ridiculous earmuffs, but her mass of thick, golden brown hair was still tangled around a long, narrow face, which, at the moment, was devoid of color, natural or otherwise. He studied her features. Not pretty, exactly, but with eyes that tilted slightly and a full mouth that could be described as lush, intriguing.

That mouth suddenly puckering in disapproval, Laurel unzipped her olive drab jacket and removed it to reveal a sweatshirt that caught his complete attention. From a deep blue background gazed two sets of mesmerizing eyes. Wolves' eyes. He recognized the design as the signature of WRIN, Wolf Recovery Information Network, a volunteer organization that disseminated information about wolves to the public in addition to helping with tracking studies.

"Why are you doing this?" Laurel's sudden demand made him start.

"This? You mean bringing my..." he couldn't squeeze the word *father* past his lips "...*him* to an emergency room for treatment? I'd do that for *any* stranger in trouble." Exactly what Raymond McKenna was to him.

"You're *not* his son. I *know* Donovan Wilde and you're not him."

"If you say so."

His words sounded calm enough, though the hair on his scalp ruffed. He didn't think she was trying to screw him around. Judging from her expression, she believed what she was saying. And her wearing that sweatshirt...

So what was *he* supposed to believe? That someone was pretending to be him? To what end?

This wasn't making any sense.

"You *can't* be Donovan," Laurel muttered, as if she were trying to convince herself.

Not knowing why he did so, Donovan produced his wallet and threw it at her. She started but nevertheless caught it. White-knuckled, she unfolded the leather billfold and pulled out his identification.

He watched her with interest.

Disbelief turned to resignation as she carefully checked over each piece—his driver's license twice. Seeming both stunned and convinced, Laurel fumbled with the cards, but her shaking hands wouldn't fit them back where they belonged.

His own gut tightening, Donovan left his chair and took the damned things from her, his fingers brushing hers in the process. Her head snapped up and she jerked back as if he'd shocked her. Electrified himself, he nevertheless held his ground.

"Satisfied?" he growled at her.

"No, not at all." Laurel blinked and her eyes suddenly shone with unshed tears. In a small voice, she added, "But I do believe you."

He waited for more. Questions. Explanations. But she turned inward, shutting him out.

Respecting her need for privacy, putting off the demands he'd like to make of her, Donovan retreated. But he couldn't keep himself from worrying about an old man who should mean nothing to him.

Couldn't keep his mind from pressing for answers. *What the hell was going on?*

LAUREL COULDN'T BE more stunned.

The *real* Donovan. There he was, bigger than life. Hers had been a fake.

No wonder his family hadn't recognized the man she'd described as being one of their own. And no wonder the real Donovan had seemed so familiar. He was a leaner, meaner version of his older half brother Skelly.

She didn't think he'd take that as a compliment, not when he wouldn't even call the congressman his father. He'd intimated they were strangers, and it seemed likely they were. Yet, thinking his younger son was in trouble, Raymond had rushed to the rescue. Now *he* was the one in trouble…possibly fighting for his life.

And it was *her* fault.

The real Donovan didn't need any rescuing as far as she could see. From the looks of him, he could handle anything that came his way.

If she hadn't sought out the McKennas, this disaster would have been averted. Raymond would have had a wonderful evening with his family and now would be in his own bed rather than in a hospital.

All her fault…

Guilt eating at her, she mentally removed herself from the situation and drifted through a cottony fog. She was aware of Donovan rising and crossing to the counter where Sophie asked him questions and he filled in a form.

At some point, he commandeered a phone.

And all the while, she wondered how she could have been fooled so badly. How she could have been so horribly mistaken.

She retreated further, thinking of nothing at all, not snapping out of it until the sounds of activity broke through the fog sometime later. She blinked. Donovan was sitting across from her once more, his face shadowed by a thick lock of long blue-black hair that escaped its leather binding. One of the nurses was going over something in the chart with the admitting clerk, while the physician was approaching the waiting area, rubbing his balding head.

Donovan flew to his feet. "Dr. Graves, how is he?"

"The wound wasn't as serious as it could have been. Your father must have thrown his arm in front of his head to protect himself."

Just as she'd surmised. "He's all right, then." She breathed a sigh of relief.

"We hope so. He hasn't come around yet, though," the physician said, giving Laurel the impression that he should already have done so. "He's still out from that blow to the head."

"Blow?" Donovan bellowed. "How could I have missed that?"

"You're sure someone actually hit him in the head?" Laurel asked, thinking of Raymond's raised voice.

Dr. Graves furrowed his brow. "How else..."

"The car," she said. "A deer bounded across our

path, and when he swerved to avoid it, we landed in a culvert. He was bleeding a bit, but he said he was all right. That's when he set out on foot.''

"Hmm. That *could* be the source of his problem."

"Then why didn't he pass out in the first place?" Donovan demanded.

"Head wounds can be unpredictable. For example, he could come to any moment."

"What if he doesn't? How long could he stay under?"

"Indefinitely, I'm afraid."

Her relief short-lived, Laurel closed her eyes and prayed that wouldn't happen.

"In the meantime," the physician continued, "I'll have to ask you to stay long enough to talk to someone from the sheriff's office. They'll try to find the animal that did this so we can make certain it's healthy."

Healthy...

No *healthy* wolf had ever attacked anyone on this continent... But what if one of the wolves in the area wasn't healthy? Laurel thought. What if it was rabid?

Noting Donovan's clenched jaw, she wondered if he was thinking along similar lines. If so, he didn't voice his opinion, and she could hardly blame him. Raymond had said he lived in the woods with his wolves....

Dr. Graves gave Donovan permission to visit his father for a few minutes. He hesitated long enough that she thought he might demur. But in the end, he nodded and went along with the physician.

Thinking about animals made her remember her own.

The first time they'd stopped for gas, she'd made a quick call to her neighbor Jack, who'd promised to feed all and walk the dogs before bed and in the morning. She'd assumed she'd be home by midday, but now that was out of the question. She wasn't even certain of how she'd get back to Chicago. Or when. She couldn't think about leaving before knowing Raymond would be all right.

Hoping Jack would forgive her for waking him before dawn, she placed another call. Between yawns, he agreed to take care of her animals until further notice.

Laurel strayed back to the waiting area but was too keyed up to sit. She didn't have long to wait alone, however. Within minutes, the law arrived even as Donovan returned, his expression grim.

Heart skipping a beat, she focused on him. "He's…"

"The same," Donovan finished for her. He turned to the uniform.

The middle-aged lawman introduced himself. "Deputy Sheriff Ralf Baedecker here. I need to ask you two some questions."

"Of course," Laurel said.

He quickly jotted down the basics—names and addresses—then went for the details. His manner was open and encouraging, easing Laurel into the story. Without going into why, she told him they'd set out to find the congressman's son. She told him about the deer and their crash. About hearing the congressman's voice followed by his shout of alarm.

"So, he was arguing with someone?"

"I'm not sure. I mean, he sounded…well, agitated…but I never heard a second person."

"Go on."

"I raced off and literally tripped over his body. That's when Donovan showed up, just in time to help."

The smile never left the deputy's lips when he glanced at Donovan. "Great timing. You're the congressman's son."

"So to speak."

"And you just what…happened to be strolling by in the middle of the night?"

"Is there some law against it?"

Tension crackled between the two men, making her shift in her chair.

"Touchy young fella, aren't you? Donovan Wilde. Familiar." He concentrated a moment before his brow cleared. "You're involved in the wolf recovery program in these parts."

Donovan nodded. "I trap and collar the animals, then track their movements."

Exactly what *her* Donovan had said.

Baedecker clucked. "This is going to reflect badly on the program, I'm afraid. And we're gonna need your cooperation."

"How so?"

"To trap the wolf that attacked your father, of course."

"Wolves don't attack humans."

"Apparently one did now."

"I know my wolves," Donovan growled.

"Then what's *your* theory?"

"I don't have one…yet."

The deputy made some more notes, then rose. "I'll be talking to the sheriff about this, young fella. Sorry to say that when it comes to predators—whether the two-footed or four-footed variety—he's not one to let things slide." He nodded to Laurel. "Miss."

Jaw clenched, Donovan glared at the deputy as he sauntered away. "Get your things," he said without looking at her. "We're leaving."

"What about your family? Don't you think we should call them about your…Congressman Mc-Kenna?"

He was pulling on his jacket. "I already called my mother." He made it sound as if he had no one else. "She volunteered to notify his family." Grabbing his headgear, he stalked toward the exit.

Laurel bit back a harsh response. Having no clue as to the source of what appeared to be a mutual animosity, she should give him the benefit of the doubt. The circumstances made doing so difficult, however. Raymond McKenna *was* his father. What was wrong with Donovan? Why couldn't he make peace with the man before it was too late?

Thinking about the loved ones she'd lost too early in her own life made her move fast. She wanted out of the hospital and *now*. She pulled on her jacket and flew after him into the breaking dawn.

Some serious snow had piled up. Donovan was clearing the windows on the Tracker. As she approached the truck, she noticed something she'd missed earlier—his personalized license plate, an image of a timber wolf and the letters W-I-L-D-E. Another testimony to the way she'd been fooled.

Without a word, she climbed into the passenger seat.

If she expected him to grill her, she had a long wait. As he drove back the way they'd come, Donovan took refuge in a sullen silence, leaving her to her own thoughts.

Only sometime later, when they turned off the highway and into the woods, did he startle her by suddenly asking, "Why didn't you tell the deputy everything?"

"What do you imagine I left out?"

He gave her a searing glance. "That I'm not the Donovan you came here to find."

Chapter Three

"What does it matter?" Laurel asked, sounding a little too offhand.

"It must matter to *you* or you wouldn't be here," Donovan returned. She radiated tension. "And it must matter to *him* or he wouldn't have come running to northern Wisconsin in the middle of the night."

"You matter to him, not some stranger. You're his son."

"By whose standards?"

"Obviously not yours. How high are they?" she demanded. "Could anyone meet them?"

Her questions ticked him off.

She knew nothing about what he'd gone through before choosing not to care. Considering her attitude, she'd probably been raised in the perfect, all-American family. Two parents, two-point-five kids, a station wagon and a dog.

"Yeah. Someone could meet my standards," he informed her. "A man who treated me like his son…rather than like his big mistake."

That shut Laurel's mouth for a moment. But Donovan didn't want her quiet. Not now. *Now* he wanted answers. And he meant to get them.

"So, this guy who's using my name, what's he to you?"

"Nothing. Not anymore."

The quaver in her voice spoke volumes. Donovan almost felt sorry for her when he continued to probe. "But he *was* something."

"I believed so...fool that I am."

"And what exactly made you come running after him?"

She hesitated a moment, then, voice sharp with pain, said, "I thought he was in some kind of trouble. He disappeared. So I went to your father, to see if he knew where you...rather, his supposed son...was."

Donovan couldn't stop the harsh laugh from escaping him. "As if the old man keeps track of me."

"I think he might."

"Probably the only reason he even knows where I am is because my mother told him I'd taken the job here."

As much as he would have preferred to keep moving, he'd returned to familiar territory because of his mother. She was his only family...as he was hers. She wasn't getting any younger. He had to keep an eye on her, make sure she was okay. If only she'd marry Josh, a man who'd been mooning over her for years, he would sleep easier. She deserved a husband who loved and wanted to do for her. The husband she'd never had...

"He knew you were in Idaho before this," Laurel was saying, pursuing the topic.

"But I didn't know he knew. Enough said?" He'd

never heard from the man, but obviously his mother was at work again. Instigating. Still trying to make them accept each other after all these years. "But that's not the point. We were talking about you and why you're here."

"Your cousin Keelin sensed you were in trouble."

Keelin. The one who'd come all the way from Ireland to reconcile her aunt and uncle with her father. Aileen had talked about Keelin when she'd called, pleading with him to come with them to the McKenna family reunion in Ireland. As if he'd voluntarily put himself in such a lousy situation. He wasn't a McKenna and never would be.

"I've never even met Keelin!" he said gruffly.

Not that it stopped her.

"She seemed very certain. Something to do with the family legacy. She was so upset, that your father practically flew out of the house to come after you."

That news gave him pause. "Why...what would she even know about me?"

"Nothing specific. Donovan—the imposter—told me she has the sight. Her husband mentioned it, as well, last night. Keelin said she didn't have to see this. She knew it was the family legacy at work."

"One little hitch. *I* haven't really disappeared...the reason you approached them."

"But Skelly agreed that you were next in line," Laurel insisted. "And on the way up here, the congressman told me his mother left a legacy of the heart to her grandchildren, but that it went hand in hand with danger. And he cited Skelly and your cousins Keelin and Kathleen as proof. They all faced some terrible danger."

"But I'm not the one in trouble, am I?"

If there was one thing Donovan mourned, it was not having had the chance to meet the one McKenna who'd truly cared about him. His grandmother Moira had always written to him with such love, from the time he was a child. And he'd faithfully written to her in return, right up to her death. Afterward, he'd received a final letter which he still treasured...her last wishes for him and her other grandchildren.

...Dreams are not always tangible things, but more often are born in the heart. Act selflessly in another's behalf, and my legacy will be yours...

And he'd turned thirty-three—the magic age for this to occur, according to his grandmother—nearly two weeks before.

Donovan shook his head. "If you believe in such nonsense." Despite his words, he envisioned yellow eyes staring at him from the dark.

"The rest of your family believes. And they're all concerned about you."

"Right. I can just see Skelly worrying."

His older brother hated his guts. Skelly had been pure hell to be around. As a teenager, he'd even tried beating the tar out of him. Skelly McKenna had seriously underestimated his father's bastard....

Laurel was sitting forward, staring out the windshield. "I think we should have come upon the congressman's car by now. I hope we didn't pass it."

"I doubt we could have missed it. Do you have any idea of the distance to the highway?"

"Not exactly, but it was a ways in, not too far from where you found us, actually. Before he set off on foot, he said we were near your cabin."

Donovan wondered how his father would even know where to look for him, considering he lived in the middle of nowhere. As they neared his place, they passed no vehicle, off-road or otherwise.

"Maybe the service towed it in," Laurel said. "I used the car cell phone to call for help, and I left the keys in the ignition. Could they have just taken it?"

"Sounds likely. Whoever came out probably figured you found shelter for the night."

"I guess I'll have to make another call then."

"Right." Knowing she wouldn't be happy about this, he said, "Later."

"Why later?"

"I don't know about you, but I need some sleep, and we'll have to go into town to find a telephone."

"You could take me there and just leave me. I'm perfectly capable of finding a telephone on my own."

"Then what?"

"I suppose I'll have to get a room."

Donovan laughed. "Where do you propose to do that?"

"In a motel?"

"You overestimate the sophistication of Iron Lake. We do have one motel, but it's seasonal. Owners go to Florida for the winter. You'd be lucky to find someone willing to rent you a room for the night."

"I may be staying for more than a night," she said, throwing him for a loop.

"Why? You think you're going to find this Donovan of yours?"

"He's not *my* Donovan, but, yes, I'd like to find him." Some of the hurt had left her voice to be replaced by steel. "But, primarily, I'm thinking of your father...even if you aren't."

Donovan clenched his jaw before he could say something cruel in return. If she wanted to waste her time, that was her business. But she wasn't going to waste his. Nor would he jump to her tune. For the moment, she'd take what he was willing to give her, or she could walk to town.

That settled in his mind, he turned down the old logging road.

THE WATCHER'S GUT did a jig when the Tracker pulled in. Hours of waiting for the prey to return finally paid off.

The wolfman slid out from behind the wheel. Even as his moccasins hit the fresh snow, he stopped and peered around, then lifted his head as if sniffing out danger. Suspicion radiated from him, as well it should.

But he wouldn't see or smell a thing out of place. The thicket of trees and bushes provided ample camouflage, and unless Wilde knew exactly where to look...

The other door opened to reveal his passenger. What was *she* doing here and where was the old man?

Fear filtered through other equally strong emotions, and a sense of self-preservation took precedence. The plan needed to be recalculated.

The wolfman had been the target!

What if the old man was dead when he hadn't even been part of the original equation?

Life didn't always work out the way one imagined

it would.

Obviously, neither did death...

RESIGNED TO HER situation, too tired to argue, Laurel was actually glad when the trip ended where it had begun. Daylight allowed her to see what she hadn't been able to the night before: Donovan's home.

Set back a bit from the road, the log structure perched beneath a ring of decades-old pine trees. Picture-postcard perfect with its snow-covered roof, stacks of cut wood snugged on either side of the door, the cabin reminded her of an article she'd read on the ideal honeymoon getaway.

As they approached on foot, she also noticed the antenna for his radio—his not having a telephone a reminder of how far from civilization they were.

"Did you build this yourself?"

"You give me too much credit. I'm Trapper Dan, remember? Not Paul Bunyan."

If she didn't know better, she might think he had a sense of humor.

Donovan climbed the two steps to the porch, stamped his feet and cleared the remainder of the snow from the soles of his moccasins using the boot scraper next to the door. Laurel gazed around in awe of the view. His home was set in the midst of a winter wonderland. She could definitely understand the attraction of living out here in God's country.

That he didn't use a key to enter didn't surprise her. City-paranoid about such things, she knew country folk had a more relaxed attitude. Besides which, the cabin was so isolated that, to raid it, someone would first have to know of its existence. She doubted many people did.

And yet, as she stepped onto the porch, the very thought shot a chill straight up her spine. She whipped around and stared out again, the majestic beauty suddenly shadowed with menace. The oddest feeling ambushed her…as if someone were watching. Breath catching in her throat, she squinted against the bright sun's glare, searching the landscape.

"Hey, you're letting the cold in!" her host growled.

Starting, putting down her spooky feeling to an overactive imagination, she muttered, "Sorry," and rushed to the door, glancing back only once before entering.

Donovan was shoving a log into the Franklin stove that dominated the center of the spacious room. His heating unit set the tone for the rest of the cabin. The walls were exposed logs rather than plaster, and the floor was composed of a solid wood planking. The scent of pine hung heavy on the air, bringing the outdoors inside.

"All the comforts of home." Donovan turned on his radio, filling the cabin with a low hum and crackles of static. "You're going to overheat if you don't get rid of that jacket. You can hang it over there."

He'd already draped his outerwear on one of the pegs next to the door and had begun removing a second layer.

"An electric stove," she murmured, glancing at the narrow appliance. "And a real refrigerator. I thought you didn't get utilities out here?"

"I don't."

"So do you have your own generator? Or do you

keep a couple dozen squirrels and raccoons chasing each other on a gigantic wheel?''

Not dignifying her questions with a response, he couldn't have been more straight-faced.

The heat made her yawn. She divested herself of her jacket and hung it on the peg next to his, then wandered through the living space.

The furniture was rugged yet comfortable look-ing—the couch a rustic wood frame with cushions, their woven coverings in a deep green-and-black north woods pattern. One corner held a dining nook of matching materials. Monopolizing the other side of the room was a work area. A large crude table was banked by half a wall of wooden cabinetry, extending to another outside door. At the near end sat the radio transmitter that could connect him at least to some parts of the civilized world.

''That's the bathroom, such as it is.'' Donovan in-dicated the first door on the other side of the cooking area. ''The bedroom's next to it. I suggest you keep the door open if you want to stay warm.''

He was offering her his own bed? Surprised by the unexpected generosity, she asked, ''What about you?''

''That an invitation?''

He was down to his long underwear—the top part, anyway. Red flannel printed with black silhouettes of wolves, their noses raised to the sky, poked out of the well-worn jeans that had been covered by his deer-hide pants. Unable to believe Donovan was capable of whimsy, she couldn't keep herself from staring at the undershirt.

He cleared his throat. "My mother's Christmas present," he muttered.

"Oh." She enjoyed his discomfiture.

The flannel did nothing to hide the lines of his torso or the breadth of his shoulders. And the jeans showed off his lean, long legs and hugged a butt and thighs taut with muscle. She tore her eyes away from the impressive sight and met his amber gaze, equally intent on her. He seemed to be waiting for something.

"Uh, about that invitation thing..." she croaked. "...I merely meant the couch seems a bit short for you."

He stared a bit longer, then grunted, "It'll do." With that, he turned his back to her.

Shut out again.

HIS MIND ON OVERLOAD, Donovan slept in fits and starts.

Thoughts too much to process, he dozed.

Dreams too disturbing, he awakened.

He'd gotten through the crisis with his father by not thinking too deeply on the whys and wherefores. Now, knowing the chain of events that had brought the old man to his neck of the woods, they plagued him.

A fake Donovan.

Someone pretending to *be* him. Why?

To set up his father? A political enemy, perhaps? Someone who wanted Congressman Raymond McKenna out of the way?

A theory that rang false.

The sequence of events couldn't have been planned so perfectly. Perhaps there was no connection at all.

And yet...

Why would a stranger approach Laurel, fake his identity and tell her all about a family that wasn't his?

But the whys and wherefores faded in significance when compared to the consequence of his father's wild-goose chase: a hospital bed, one from which he might never rise...

He hadn't been able to stay in that claustrophobia-producing room for long, hadn't been able to stand the sight of a man whose power had been stripped so completely that he was dependent on machines to see to his needs.

The man who had sired him, who had been the lifelong focus of his rage, had been reduced to nothing more than a shell.

It made him want to weep.

THE AROMA OF hundred-proof coffee tantalized Laurel awake. Groaning, she reached out, blindly searching for a cat to fondle...the lack of a fur creature her first clue that something was amiss.

Opening her eyes gave her a rude shock. The room was foreign to her. It took a moment to remember where she was. And why.

Had the congressman awakened yet? she wondered. Without a telephone, how would they know?

"Donovan?"

No answer.

She stumbled out of bed and to the bathroom, where she splashed her face with copious amounts of cold water, enough to clear her head a bit. Squinting at her watch informed her noon was fast approaching.

Following her nose to the coffeepot on the stove,

Laurel filled a mug and gulped down half the lukewarm contents. Better. No country coffee for the
wolfman, thank goodness. Full-bodied, packed with
caffeine, it did the trick, vaporizing the remnants of
sleep from her brain.

And still no Donovan.

His things no longer hung from the peg next to the
door. Unwilling to sit around twiddling her thumbs
until he returned, Laurel decided to find him. Still
dressed, she pulled on her boots and jacket, secured
earmuffs to her head and gloves to her hands. If leaving the warmth of the cabin was disagreeable, at least
the sun's brilliance and a lack of wind made the cold
tolerable.

Following the trail left by Donovan's snowshoes
was easy enough—at least she knew what direction
to take. Actually getting from point *A* to point *B* was
another matter. Even placing her feet directly on his
trail didn't help. The snow wasn't packed, and as had
happened the night before, she kept breaking through
the top crust.

To her relief, Donovan hadn't gone far. She spotted
him across the open field, his destination chillingly
familiar. He was crouching over the area where his
father had fallen. Barely an impression left from a
body, she noted. As she stopped to catch her breath
several yards behind him, he was gently brushing
away new snow from a smaller depression.

He made no sign that he knew she was there, but
when he said, "The drift covered the prints too well,"
she knew he had sensed her presence.

"Trying to convince yourself that your wolves are

innocent?'' Which she only hoped they were…and feared they weren't.

"I don't need convincing. I know what I know."

"Then what are you looking for?"

Continuing with his task, he said, "Proof that he wasn't alone out here."

He. Why couldn't he just say the word *father?*

So, he was looking for tracks made by a person rather than by an animal.

"Footprints," Laurel murmured. "What if…" She started. "Of course they weren't yours."

"What weren't?"

The moments before finding Donovan's father were clear in her mind. "I followed the congressman's prints from the car. At some point, they crossed another set."

Donovan straightened. "And you didn't think this important enough to mention last night?"

She made allowances for his accusing tone. "I assumed the second set belonged to you…actually, the man I thought was you…but you were wearing snowshoes. Maybe it's nothing…I mean, who's to say if those tracks weren't there from earlier in the day or even from another day altogether—"

"Whoa! Save your breath and just show me."

Laurel squinted out at the copse of trees, looking for the trailhead. "Over there."

Donovan was already off and running, so to speak, and she was left behind to struggle with the knee-deep snow.

"If you want me to keep up with you," she loudly complained, "you'll have to find me a pair of snowshoes!"

"You won't be around long enough to make use of them."

Struggling to keep up, Laurel muttered, "Don't be too sure of that."

In the end, Donovan waited for her at the edge of the woods, and once on the packed base, his advantage lessened. She noted the farther they went into the woods, the less new snow had drifted over the trail. She was beginning to spot some impressions herself.

They didn't have far to go before Donovan slowed and stooped to examine a pretty well-defined print. No ridges for traction. He ran his fingers lightly over the smooth impression, the type made by a leather sole. The congressman had been wearing city shoes.

Checking a second, smaller print with ridges, he said, "Show me the bottom of your boot."

Bracing a hand on a tree trunk for balance, she let him examine the rubber lug sole that gave her traction on slippery surfaces. She knew he was comparing the tread on her boot to the print on the trail.

When he let go, she asked, "Mine?"

"Yours."

Laurel scrutinized Donovan as he carefully examined the area. Expression intent, he didn't seem to notice. With his picturesque headgear and deerskin garments, he was a throwback to another century. And yet, he appeared completely comfortable in the role...and with himself. No trace of insecurity. No troubled air beneath the resolute demeanor.

The real Donovan was a man's man with shoulders broad enough to lean on.

Not like the man who'd purported to be Donovan

Wilde, she thought, a wave of resentment sweeping through her.

What purpose had his impersonation served other than to make a fool of her? Rather, she'd made a fool of herself getting so involved with someone she'd obviously misread. She could no longer trust her own instincts. Her only consolation was that she hadn't actually accepted his proposal of marriage.

If she'd said yes, would the fake Donovan have gone through with a bogus wedding ceremony?

The possible repercussions alarmed her....

"Hmm, what have we here?" Donovan was muttering to himself. "A different pattern in the tread."

He brushed a bit of loose snow from an imprint larger than hers. As he examined it more closely, his expression suddenly hardened.

"What is it?" she asked.

Totally absorbed, he moved on, checked another print and then another, as if she weren't there.

"So, say something already," she demanded. "Were they walking together or what?"

He shook his head. "Can't be certain...not of that."

Exasperated, she asked, "Could you be any less clear?"

Rising, he stared at her. Rather, *through* her was more like it. She could practically see the wheels turning inside his head, drawing conclusions.

"That tread..." he said at last, "...it *is* the same."

He met her gaze. Finally, he'd made a connection.

But what she saw in his eyes made her tremble inside.

INSTINCT DROVE Donovan to find the point where the two sets of prints first met. His gut felt tight as a drum.

"Am I invisible or what? Or do you make a habit of ignoring everyone like this?"

Laurel's shrill complaint got through to him. He stopped short and gave her his full attention, questioning her with raised eyebrows.

Which appeared to mollify her, made her settle her prickly feathers.

In a less hostile tone, she asked, "So, are you going to interpret that mysterious comment or just leave me hanging?

"I thought I made it clear that I've seen that same print before."

"But when? And where?"

"More than once over the past several weeks." They belonged to the intruder whose presence he'd detected even if he hadn't been able to apprehend the person. Sometimes the intruder had worn snowshoes, other times the boots that had left this print. "Near the cabin. The old wolf den. One of the trap sites."

He'd suspected the trespasser was someone who had it in for the wolves. While the local emotional climate for wolf recovery was on the whole tolerant, there were enough people who still thought the only good wolf was a dead one. Several locals had been up in arms when a sickly cow had been found dead, its throat torn open, only the week before.

Laurel cut into his thoughts. "How can you be sure the prints were made by the same person?"

Crouching, he waved her over to show her. "Look at the pattern. The center of the tread is made up of perfect diamond shapes. But not here on the left print.'' He pointed to a section that didn't match the rest—two of the diamonds were half gone, as if they'd been sliced off by something sharp, like a piece of broken glass.

''Wow, great eyes,'' Laurel said, so close her breath feathered his cheek.

''Paying attention to detail is my job.''

Caught unawares by the spark of admiration in her expression, Donovan was tempted to tell her she had great eyes, too, the compliment having nothing to do with the process at hand.

In the end he rose, purposely casual, setting his gaze to roaming the area for other, smaller prints. ''I imagine you're ready for some chow.''

''You cook, too?''

Donovan started. Laurel's expression said she was teasing him again. He couldn't fathom why she'd want to. No one else teased him. Ever. Not since he was a kid, anyway.

''I was thinking about getting some grub in town,'' he said, starting back toward the cabin. While upon awakening he'd radioed to find out about his father's unchanged condition, he didn't want to wear out his welcome with the sheriff's office. In town, he could make a proper phone call. ''And assuming word's gotten around, it wouldn't hurt to test the pulse of the locals.''

From directly behind, she asked, ''About the wolves?''

He was still scanning the rolling ground around them. ''Among other things...''

Narrowing his gaze when the tracks practically

jumped out at him, he stopped abruptly, half turning to alert Laurel, who crashed right into him. She put out a hand as if to catch herself—her fingers splaying across his chest even as he threw a steadying arm around her back.

For a moment, wrapped in each other's arms, neither spoke.

Donovan stared into Laurel's face, which reflected sudden confusion, and he wondered if the color brushing her nose and cheeks came from the cold…or from something else entirely. Something stirred in him, as well. A mutual attraction? More likely a natural urge that needed satisfying, he told himself. This one talked too much for it to be anything more. Even so, it took him a moment to let go and back off. That she appeared relieved rankled.

He forced his attention back to the reason he'd stopped. ''Take a look over there.'' Pointing, he left the trail to check things out.

Laurel followed his lead, but, voice breathy enough to make his groin tighten, she said, ''I don't see anything.''

He stooped to examine what remained of animal tracks. The prints themselves weren't clear…but the pattern was.

''Wolf?'' she asked.

He'd hoped to find sloppy tracks zigzagging from one side to the other as would be left by a dog. These traveled in too straight a path, rear prints neatly tucking into the fore. Disappointment knotted his gut.

''Wolf,'' he finally agreed.

Chapter Four

Veronica Wilde shoved the plate down on the counter in front of Joshua Harley and checked the wall clock. Ten more minutes. She'd call the hospital at two.

What she really wanted to do was get in her car and drive to Nicolet General Hospital. Then what? She wasn't family. She had no say. She was lucky the nurse would tell her anything. Thank God, Donovan had thought to give her name as a contact person.

"Ronnie, honey," Josh said, cutting through the fog she'd been in since her son's middle-of-the-night call. "I ordered a ham sandwich, not beef. And I asked for hash browns instead of French fries."

She stared down at his plate without really registering the contents. "Sorry, I'll fix it." Automatically she went to remove the food.

But Josh caught her hand and covered it with both of his own. "No need," he assured her. "But you gotta get a grip, honey."

She nodded. Josh had to be the most understanding man in the world. She'd told him about Raymond. And other than that one second when she'd caught a flash of something dark in his expression, he'd been completely supportive.

"I'll be all right," she assured him. "If only I could see him for myself…"

"And do what? Resurrect him with old memories?"

Though his words held a bite, Josh was still smiling. Veronica tried to stretch her lips, too, but the response felt wooden.

"Hey, how 'bout some more coffee?" another customer grumbled at her from the other end of the counter.

"Coming, Titus."

Veronica used the pot as a shield, keeping it between her and the people she'd known for most of her life. None of whom were as important to her right now as the man in that hospital bed.

Her son's father.

Donovan hadn't seemed too upset when he'd called to tell her that Raymond was hurt, in some kind of coma. His disregard for his own parent wasn't natural, but then his and Raymond's relationship had never been natural…had mostly been forced on them both by her.

If only things could have been different.

If only she had been the kind of woman Raymond had needed in his life.…

The outside door opened, inviting in the cold. She turned to see her son enter, a tall thin woman preceding him. Must be that Newkirk woman he'd told her about. The one who'd been with Raymond. She was still puzzling over the woman's part in the story Raymond had told her when he'd called from Chicago.

"Donny," she murmured, sweeping between tables to get to him as a low buzz swept through the café.

People stared outright at Donovan. He *was* some sight in that getup. But it wasn't his appearance that caused a stir, Veronica knew. People were used to that since he came into town regularly for supplies.

Word of the attack had already gotten around and speculation was rife. Not that most folks would dare say anything negative to her directly.

That Donovan was here at all relieved her mind a bit. He *had* to be worried about Raymond or, considering the circumstances and his distaste at being fodder for gossip, he would've avoided Iron Lake like the plague.

DONOVAN HADN'T WARNED Laurel that the Veronica of Veronica's Vittles was his mother. But the introduction when they'd entered the typical small-town eatery, with its Formica-topped counter and tables and its vinyl-covered padded stools and chairs, hadn't been necessary.

The eyes gave her away—amber, glowing, read-through-you eyes exactly like her son's. And the older woman *was* reading her between waiting on the few lunch customers who still straggled into the place.

A decade or more younger than the congressman, Veronica Wilde hadn't lost the looks that must have captivated her lover. Her body appeared slim and strong. Minimal silver threaded her heavy blue-black hair that she'd twisted into an artful coil at the base of her neck. More exotic than conventionally beautiful, her features remained unmarred by time but for a few tiny lines at the outer edges of her almond-shaped eyes.

Laurel suspected a Native American ancestry somewhere in Veronica's background…and therefore in Donovan's, as well.

As they ate the huge midday breakfast his mother had cooked for them, she noted that Veronica made a telephone call before finally settling at the counter. There she spoke with a man who'd been present before they'd arrived. Salt-and-pepper hair topped a pleasant, sun-lined face, and a blue work shirt and pants enveloped a physically fit if age-thickened body. His lunch plate long ago pushed to the side, he seemed to be drinking a bottomless cup of coffee.

Laurel suspected the man's interest lay more in the proprietress than in the contents of his cup.

"That's Josh Harley, owner of the local garage and auto parts store," Donovan told her. "Josh is a long time friend of the family."

From his expression as he gazed at Veronica, Laurel gathered Josh was interested in more than simple friendship. "How long?" she asked, thinking of his evident infatuation.

"Ever since I can remember. He taught me how to fish. How to start a campfire. And to find my direction by reading the stars."

"Guy things." Obviously, he'd missed her drift. "Sounds like you two bonded."

Donovan didn't answer. Big surprise. But from his suddenly tense expression, she guessed she'd struck a nerve. He appeared…almost guilty. Curious. She couldn't imagine this man feeling guilt over anything.

She noticed that Veronica split her attention between Josh and them. And even as they finished their meal, the older woman joined them, seeming ready to speak her mind.

Gaze fixing Laurel to the spot, she said, "Raymond told me you came to him with some wild tale of a stranger pretending to be our son."

When Veronica glanced at Donovan as if for corroboration, he said, "It's her story."

Laurel told it quickly, succinctly, once more leaving out the more intimate details. When she finished, mother and son connected, shutting her out, the thick silence speaking volumes about the closeness of *their* relationship.

Feeling almost as if she were intruding, Laurel cleared her throat and said, "Congressman McKenna was determined to find your son to make certain he was all right. And if so, he meant to warn Donovan that something was up and that he should watch his back."

Veronica nodded. "That's pretty much what he told me when he called last night. But your story didn't make sense then and it doesn't now. Just who are you?"

The woman already knew her name, so what was she looking for?

"I don't understand."

"Are you someone important?"

"Only to a bunch of formerly homeless animals who depend on me," Laurel said truthfully.

She had no one else…nothing else…not even her fantasy of a big loving family to hold on to any longer.…

"But not to the wolves," Veronica murmured.

Laurel shook her head. "Not that I wouldn't like to be important to their survival beyond making small contributions. But my life's in Chicago. I work for the city, actually—Streets and Sanitation."

She tried not to sound defensive. Circumstances had forced her to take a good-paying, steady job that she didn't want in lieu of finishing the education that she desired. One day soon she would have the medical debts paid off, and she could decide what to do with the rest of her life. In the meantime…

"I'm an equipment driver," she explained. "Street cleaner in the summer, snowplow in the winter."

Veronica didn't even blink at her unusual background. "That's about as far from working with wolves as you can get, I guess. Then…why you?"

"I don't have a clue," Laurel said truthfully. "I don't know why he picked me or what he was up to." She still found it difficult not to think of the man she'd come to care about as Donovan. "But I sure intend to find out. If I can."

Not that she had the slightest idea of how to begin. And not that knowing would make her feel any better.

Nothing would erase her foolishness at putting all her trust in some stranger just because he'd been handsome and charming and had seemed nice. And vulnerable. She suspected she was a bit too susceptible to a hard-luck story…or wounded demeanor, in the case of her fake Donovan. Though maybe he *had* been wounded and vulnerable. Unfortunately, that hadn't made him honest.

Veronica touched her son's arm. "I called about your father while you were eating. His condition hasn't changed. Your sister's with him, though. I spoke to her. Aileen promised to call with any news…either way."

Laurel heard the slight break in her voice.

"You sound exhausted, Mom." Frowning, Donovan looked around. "Where's that guy you hired?"

"You know how it is keeping help around here. I had hopes for Billy, but in the end, he up and took off on me just like the last one. Still, I'm not the one to be fretting over."

"Neither am I," Donovan insisted, any further protest cut off as the door to the café swung open with a bang.

In strode a big red-haired, bearded man whose mouth spread into an even bigger grin when he spotted Donovan. He stalked toward their table. Something about that smile felt wrong, Laurel thought, noting the malevolence in his hazel eyes. Her instincts went on alert when he towered over them, his flesh practically quivering in delight, and Donovan's expression hardened.

"Wilde. Thought you'd like to see the weekend *Herald*." Heedless of the dishes on the table, the big man slapped down a newspaper in front of them. "Held up the presses this morning especially for you."

In complete control, Donovan glanced at the front page without so much as a blink. Laurel didn't do nearly as well when she caught a glimpse of the cartoon—a wolf with slathering jaws. The headline shouted: Wolf Attack…Congressman Down for the Count.

"That's disgusting." She glared at the man.

Donovan said, "Laurel, meet Hamilton 'Ham'

Gault—owner, publisher and editor of the local paper. I hesitate to use the word *news*. You'd think the *National Tattler* and *World Inquisitor* would be fighting over his talents."

The grin hardened. "Don't try to deny it, Wilde. Got my info first hand from the sheriff."

"Sheriff Dwyer is ahead of himself."

"Doesn't seem to think so. Your daddy was savaged by one of them damn wolves. He dies, and the recovery program is through." He barked a laugh. "Hell, it's through now. All that's left is the eulogy."

"Don't write it yet," Donovan warned him. Voice deceptively calm, he asked, "By the way, Ham, where were *you* last night?"

The newspaper man narrowed his eyes. "What? You suddenly interested in my social life?"

"I'm interested in knowing exactly how far you'd go to kill the wolf recovery program."

"You got something stuck in your craw, Wilde, spit it out."

"Those rottweilers of yours, they have pretty big jaws. Probably could take down a buck…or, for that matter, a man."

Live-wire tension crackled between them. Laurel held her breath, waiting for an explosion. The whole café seemed to be waiting. Every eye in the place was turned their way.

Red-faced, Gault managed to hang on to his temper. "I'll take that as distress over your daddy's health speaking. But I wouldn't go around bad-mouthing a pillar of this community if I were you."

Donovan merely lifted a challenging eyebrow and stared the man down.

Muttering a curse under his breath, Gault spun around and stalked out of the café, slamming the door behind him. One by one, the other diners turned their attention back to their food. The show was over.

Forehead pulled with worry, Veronica said, "He's going to cause more trouble for you, Donny."

"His specialty."

"What would the owner and publisher of a newspaper have against the recovery program?" Laurel asked him.

"Thickheadedness, pure and simple. He's a pillar, all right. Solid stone."

She shook her head. Of course she knew that kind of blind prejudice existed against the wolves, but she thought it belonged to the people who lived off the land and feared losing their animals to a predator.

"Ham Gault is the president of the local sportsman's club," Veronica said. "He's afraid there might not be enough deer for him to shoot."

"What a joke," Donovan said. "Wisconsin has several times the volume of deer the state can handle without destruction of the vegetation. Herds are kept artificially high for the hunters, who kill maybe half a million deer a year. By contrast, our hundred wolves might take down another eighteen hundred. Vehicles take out ten times that."

Veronica added, "And every winter more and more deer die of starvation."

"As part of my graduate work," Donovan continued, "I did a study about a wolf pack's encounters with deer. How many deer detected, how many got away before the wolves got near them, how many outran or outlasted the wolves and so on. They actually only manage to kill less than five percent, many of which are old, crippled or starving. Culling the less adaptable is actually healthy for the deer herd.''

''There's another reason Ham hates wolves,'' Veronica said. ''He breeds rottweilers. Last fall, when he took several dogs hunting with him, one of the young ones disappeared, never to be seen again. Though no one ever found signs of the dog's carcass, Ham swears the wolves ripped him apart and ate him.''

Though Laurel knew that to be a real possibility, the thought made her shudder.

''The dog probably had good taste and simply went and found himself a new owner.'' Donovan indicated the remains on her plate. ''If you're done, how about making that phone call?''

''Right. The congressman's car,'' Laurel clarified for the other woman. ''It had to be towed out of a culvert.''

''Get the station's location. We can pick it up now and you can drive it home. *To Chicago.*''

Not wanting to argue with Donovan in front of his mother, Laurel rose and headed for the pay phone. She had no intention of driving back to Chicago...at least not yet, not when the congressman's condition was still in question.

''Think old Ham got it on the nose, or what?'' she heard an old-timer mumble as she approached his table.

''Don't know, Nate,'' his grizzled companion returned, ''but I wouldn't want to cross Wilde myself. He's got a way with them wolves. It's like he can control them.''

She bit her tongue to keep silent. Gossip might be rife, but she guessed that was to be expected. That the wolves were his work was circumstantial. Besides, no one could control a wild wolf to his bidding. People were always afraid of what they didn't understand...and the real Donovan was certainly an enigma.

"Hey, Andrew, think he might sic one of 'em on Ham?" Nate asked.

"You heard what happened to the congressman," Andrew said speculatively. "Never any love lost between them two. Remember that time back in the seventies when the old man came to collect him...and Ronnie had to round up a search party in the middle of the night..."

The conversation faded off as she arrived at the pay phone installed on a wall covered with framed photographs. So, even as a kid, Donovan had run from Raymond. Laurel could only imagine the hurt he'd experienced. Distracted by the bizarre thought of him being vulnerable like anyone else, she checked the phone book and dialed the station. Somehow, Donovan seemed so...impenetrable.

A woman answered and Laurel inquired about the congressman's car. There was some confusion at the other end. The woman asked her to wait a minute.

Laurel passed the time by perusing the photographs. One in particular caught her attention—a young Veronica, hair plaited, throat surrounded by a quill necklace, posing with three other Native Americans, each of whom wore some article of traditional dress.

Then the owner of the service station came on-line.

Stunned at what he had to say, she headed back to the table to share it with Donovan.

But when she heard his mother say, "I want to see Raymond, Donny," she chose not to intrude.

"And I'm certain you'll do exactly as you like."

"Stop trying to sound so heartless. I know you better than that." Veronica faltered before adding, "I want you to come with me. Please."

"What makes you think *I* want to see him?"

"He's your father."

Donovan's jaw worked. "So you keep insisting. He's in good hands. Besides, Aileen's with him now. Skelly's sure to follow."

Veronica didn't say one more word, merely held her son's gaze in a meaningful way that only a mother could. At first, Laurel didn't think Donovan would give in. Then his grim expression altered. She swore he grew uneasy under his mother's scowl.

"Yeah, all right. Tomorrow after breakfast."

"What's wrong with now?"

"I have traps to check."

Laurel thought Veronica might argue further, but in the end, the older woman compromised, nodding in agreement.

"I'd better see to my customers. Tad Norton is heading for the cash register."

She rose and, seeing Laurel, gave her a speculative look as she hurried to the counter.

Then, before Laurel could sit, Donovan asked, "Ready to leave?"

"Sure." She picked up her jacket. "But forget about going for the car."

"How serious is the damage?"

"I wouldn't know." Her stomach did a jig as she added, "And neither would the service station." When she said, "It's not there," Donovan's expression reflected her own shock. "The owner's pretty hot under the collar about the situation, too. He came out and searched the road for an hour but found nothing. He accused me of wasting his time. My saying I'd make sure he was paid barely satisfied him."

"A vehicle can't just up and disappear."

"No," she said. "Not by itself, it can't."

NOW WHAT?

Expecting Donovan to grab on to the fact that the car had been stolen, to grill her about the circumstances, Laurel was surprised when he didn't even broach the subject…as if he chose to exclude her, she thought resentfully. She stared out of the passenger window as they left town. She knew he'd stuff her on the next bus south if the only one that came through Iron Lake wasn't already long gone, as he had dispassionately informed her upon leaving the cafe.

"Tomorrow morning," he'd promised, before lapsing into his customary silence.

No talk of what *she'd* do today…or where she'd sleep tonight. She guessed it was back to his place, then. Only tonight, she'd insist on taking the couch. As to his plans to put her on a bus the next morning…let him assume what he would.

When Donovan drove his mother to Nicolet General Hospital, Laurel meant to go along for the ride. If Donovan gave her flack, she'd appeal to Veronica.

She was certain the older woman would understand and champion her request.

She wanted to be there…either way.

If Raymond came to as she fervently hoped he would, Laurel wanted to see him for herself, wanted to tell him how sorry she was that she'd gotten him into this mess. She also wanted to hear the congressman's account of his assault. What had attacked him and why? Unless he'd been haranguing the animal to make it leave him be, another person had been involved in the dangerous scenario.

The same person who'd taken the car?

Her Donovan?

On the way back to the woods, she couldn't stop thinking about the man. How he'd pursued her, charmed her, wooed her. How she'd half fallen for him, if not enough to commit herself instantly. She should have known his romancing her had been too good to be true. Not the type of woman who pushed men's erotic buttons, she should have suspected some ulterior motive when he'd gone to such great lengths to see her.

Why her?

Veronica's question echoed in her mind all the way home, until the moment they left the truck for the cabin. Unfortunately, she remained clueless.

They'd barely gotten inside the door when Donovan said, "I don't have time to entertain you."

Taken aback by his rudeness, she said, "Did I ask?"

"I have work to do."

"Fine. So do it. You don't owe me any explanations."

His outer garments flung to a chair, he moved with purpose. Half out of curiosity and half wanting to annoy him, Laurel followed Donovan to the supply closet and lounged in the doorway as he gathered his equipment and supplies. He worked quickly, efficiently, appearing for all intents and purposes capable of anything he set his mind to. Intent on his preparations, he didn't seem to be aware of her. But she was certainly aware of him.

Lanky body amazingly muscular...sharp features softened by the long strands of loose blue-black hair grazing his cheekbones...large hands, surprisingly dexterous.

What would those hands feel like touching her? she wondered. Grazing her face...brushing her throat...skimming her body?

Heat smoldered along Laurel's nerves. Where had this unexpected flare of attraction come from? She wasn't even sure she liked the man. He certainly irritated her. What was she thinking? Shifting in the doorway, she decided to get out before he noticed something was wrong.

That's when she spotted the snowshoes. An extra pair hung from a peg.

No hesitation. She decided to fetch them before Donovan could forbid it, the close quarters forcing her to brush by him in the process. As her breast grazed his arm, more heat made her catch her breath.

He narrowed his gaze, his amber eyes boring into her. "What are you up to?"

Glad for the tinge of exasperation in his tone— hoping he didn't realize what was happening to her— she latched on to the snowshoes and inspected them in detail, avoiding his eyes so he couldn't read the direction of her uncomfortable thoughts.

"Hmm. One size fits all, right?" she murmured.

"What do you imagine you're going to do with those? Get yourself lost out there?"

"Not if I'm with you."

"You won't be able to keep up."

Though Laurel expected he might be correct—while she had used snowshoes at the ecology workshop, she was still a novice—snowshoes would be better than her hiking boots. Besides, she wasn't intimidated.

"I'll take my chances."

Before he could object, she slid by him again, this time holding her breath so that no part of her would touch him. Escaping the supply closet, she left the snowshoes near the front door beside his. Then she threw herself into a chair and watched while he laid things on the worktable.

"You don't have enough clothes to spend any real time outside."

An excuse to leave her behind? "It's not as cold as it was last night," she insisted. "I'll make do."

Without another word, Donovan disappeared into his bedroom, closing the door behind him.

Laurel got antsy waiting. What was he up to? If he hadn't left his knapsack on the workbench, she might suspect him of slipping off without her. The image of him clambering through a window opening while trying not to make a sound, however, produced a snort of laughter.

She found herself relaxing.

When Donovan came out of the bedroom, she saw

that he'd changed. And that he was carrying a bundle of white material. He tossed the garments to her.

"Put these on."

Reflex made her throw her hands out to catch the waffle-patterned material. Laurel swallowed hard as she realized Donovan was lending her a set of his thermal underwear.

Remembering the red undershirt he'd worn earlier, she muttered, "What, no wolves?"

Rather than respond to her goading, he said, "And you can use this, as well." He indicated a hooded jacket hanging from the peg next to his deerskins.

Laurel zipped to the bathroom where she shed her boots, jeans and sweatshirt. She slipped into the long johns, her insides feathered by an odd sensation. Desperately, she tried not to dwell on the fact that these very same garments had caressed *his* skin....

Again the provocative thoughts.

Inappropriate thoughts, Laurel told herself.

She hurried back into her clothes so Donovan wouldn't have that excuse to leave without her.

TOGETHER STILL.

They set out from the cabin even as the afternoon shadows lengthened. They didn't go far before stopping to put on their snowshoes. Binoculars afforded a closer view of her having trouble with hers. He helped her by adjusting the straps. Appearing uncomfortable, she concentrated on cuffing sleeves that hung too long over her fingers and pulling up the hood of the obviously borrowed jacket.

Once ready, they headed north, no doubt to check the traps.

What was she doing, hanging around, following him everywhere? Why hadn't she gone back where she belonged so things could go according to schedule?

She didn't know Wilde…how dangerous he could be. How unthinkingly cruel. There had to be a reason for her hanging around. Had she witnessed more than she should have?

The thought gave pause.

She'd have to be dealt with, too, then. Gotten rid of and as soon as possible. But how?

The leather pouch held an answer….

Once they snowshoed out of sight, the cabin was fair game. A little too close for comfort, perhaps, but there was a first time for everything.

Chapter Five

Laurel was gutsy. Donovan would grant her that. She could have stayed behind and relaxed near the warmth of the stove. Instead, she chanced frostbite, exhaustion and sore muscles by trailing after him.

Why?

Though he got no complaints, he knew the unaccustomed physical exertion wasn't easy for her. She'd caught up to him when he'd checked the first trap that, unfortunately, had gone undisturbed. Now she was straggling behind again. From the amplitude of her labored breathing, he figured twenty yards, give or take a few. But no matter how quickly he moved, she somehow managed to stay within shouting distance.

While he'd like to discourage her, he really didn't want to lose her out here in the middle of nowhere. That would only make more work for him, since he'd then have to be a one-man rescue party.

Why was Laurel so reluctant to go home?

She should be more than happy to wash her hands of a difficult situation. To get out while she could. To the contrary, she seemed to be digging in her heels.

He had to admire that about her. It wasn't just a matter of her tenacity, either. He didn't know many women—or men, for that matter—who put principle before their own comfort, creature or otherwise. His gut told him that, if he wanted Laurel Newkirk out of his hair, he'd have to physically wrestle her onto that morning bus. Undoubtedly, she'd go kicking and screaming....

A dark spot in the snow distracted him from thoughts about the woman. He left the trail to check it out. From the color, as well as the fur and bone content, scat could tell him about a wolf's health and what it was eating.

He was assessing the droppings when a breathless Laurel caught up to him, gasping, "Wolf?"

"Nope. Too small. Probably coyote."

He glanced up. Her hood was cocked back, her face flushed becomingly. The workout was helping to relieve the stress that had previously tautened her features. Now they were softer. Prettier. Exhausted.

Rising, he was tempted to push on immediately anyway. Then, again, if she collapsed, he'd have to carry her back to the cabin. Which brought him to a whole new chain of considerations having to do with holding the woman in his arms....

Suddenly irritated that he had to accommodate another person at all, he asked, "Do you just attract trouble or do you go around looking for it?"

Her jaw dropped at his attack, but she blinked only once before saying, "Why, I pay to have trouble come to me. That way, my life's just one continuing riot after another."

She was quick on her feet mentally—if not on

snowshoes—Donovan realized. And while she was being sarcastic, he sensed she was covering a more vulnerable part of herself, one she didn't want him to see. So he couldn't figure out just how alone she might be?

Alone.

Now that would make sense. A reason to take a man at face value and get involved without looking too closely. Whoever had been posing as him was a predator. A lonely woman wouldn't have stood a chance against a charming con man. He'd give anything to know what, exactly, the bastard had been after.

"So, this is…what?" he prodded, hell-bent on provoking her. "A welcome change for you? Too exciting to give up and go home?" Where she should be anyway.

Laurel visibly bristled, blue eyes shooting sparks at him. "Did anyone ever mistakenly tell you that you have people skills?"

"I'm better with animals."

"I'm pretty good with both. And, despite *your* studied disinterest, *I'm* not comfortable going off and leaving your father in a coma."

Studied disinterest? Donovan clenched his jaw. She thought he had to work at it?

"The congressman isn't your responsibility."

"In a way, he is. If I hadn't gone running to him, he would never have come running to find *you.*"

"He always did what was best for himself, which means for his political career." A lesson he'd learned at his father's knee. "He operates on his own agenda. Whatever is most expedient—"

"Expedient!" she echoed, cutting him off. "He was thinking of *you!*"

Donovan wouldn't trust himself to believe that. Not again. "You don't know him like I do."

He started off back toward the trail. This time, Laurel followed so closely they could practically share a pair of snowshoes.

"I don't think you know your father at all," she taunted. "I'm not sure you ever wanted to."

"You know nothing about it," he said coldly. "There was a time—"

"Past tense," Laurel interrupted. "When you were a kid, right? Kids don't always see the big picture. They tend to run away from their problems."

What did she know about his running away? Or why it had come to that?

"You can't compare your life to mine."

"You're right on that account. I have no one. You have a whole family if only you'd stoop to recognize them." She paused to catch her breath. Her next words stopped him in his tracks. "I lost the only people who mattered in my life."

So Laurel really was alone.

"And you're throwing your family away," she added, losing the sympathy factor.

He whirled on her. "You're assuming they have some use for me."

"And you're assuming they don't." She took a deep breath, as if to calm herself. "Do you see everything in black and white? Either things have to be a certain way—the way *you* think they ought to be—or forget it?"

A criticism he'd heard once too often.

"You have a problem with ethics—my distinguishing between right and wrong?" he demanded.

"I have a problem with people who can't see shades of gray, Donovan. I don't know anyone who's perfect. Or anyone who's all bad."

INCLUDING HER IMPOSTER, Laurel thought, trailing a silent Donovan once more.

After glowering at her, the wolfman had given her his back and had taken off more speedily than before. At first determined to keep up, she'd forced her legs to go faster, but it wasn't long before her muscles burned with the effort. Knowing she'd never get back to the cabin on her own steam if she kept up this pace, she slowed a bit and fell behind. His ploys to discourage her weren't going to work.

Not wanting to dwell on the warped psyche of a man who churned her insides, Laurel steered her thoughts back to the other Donovan.

Her Donovan.

She had seen good in the man, or she wouldn't have given him the time of day. She also recognized a troubled soul when she met one. Her Donovan certainly had been that. Not enough reason to stop her from getting involved; more than enough reason to keep her from committing herself.

The real Donovan, too, was troubled, if not in the same way.

Despite the family and self-imposed isolation issues he needed to work on, he'd developed a formidable personality, a sense of self that made him comfortable with who he was. He needed no one, as he so staunchly illustrated by the widening gap between them. He was content within himself in a way she could never be.

Desperately missing what fate had stolen from her, she couldn't understand a man who thrust away the very thing she longed to regain.

Laurel needed people. Contact. Warmth. A sense of connection. A *family*. Things that she'd lost through no fault of her own. She'd tried her best to save them—first her mother from cancer, then her grandmother from the frailties and illnesses that came with age—but some things were beyond her abilities or understanding.

In trying to patch the hole in her life as best she could for the past half-dozen years, she filled her days with work and friends and meaningful interests. Not to mention the animals—and sometimes even human beings—she rescued.

That last thought jarred her.

Had that been what had attracted her to the man who'd wrongfully introduced himself as Donovan Wilde?

That he'd needed rescuing?

In return…could that also be why he'd chosen *her?*

An answer to Veronica's pointed question…

Before Laurel could assimilate the startling notion, she realized Donovan had gone off-trail again and hadn't even warned her. Gasping for breath, she stopped and peered around until she spotted snowshoe tracks leading to a stand of cedars.

She called "Donovan!" even knowing he wouldn't answer, after which she set off to play catch up.

Surely he wouldn't actually let her get lost and wouldn't leave her alone in these woods. Though she tried to convince herself, she wasn't so certain. Panic was setting in before she caught up to him near a streambed, where a trickle of water still flowed, albeit along a path of ice.

Knapsack set against some fallen trees at the edge of a small clearing, the wolfman crouched, shoulders taut, gaze unfocused.

"Makes no sense." He was muttering and shaking his head. "What the hell happened here?"

"You tell me."

Donovan started. But when he straightened, he gave no sign that she'd caught him unawares.

"So, what did you find?" she asked.

"It's what I didn't find. The trap I set here is gone."

"Then you got one of the wolves," she said excitedly.

The animal must have pulled the thing free and dragged it off. The humanely designed leghold trap was made to do just that, she knew from the wolf ecology workshop. It could be dragged rather than snapped if the wolf lunged hard. The grapples would then catch on brush or logs elsewhere.

She had the weirdest feeling about Donovan's reaction, though. "We'd better find him, right?"

"How?" He shook his head. "There'd have to be signs...a trail of some kind."

Knowing the trap would have been buried—in this season, merely under the snow—she scrutinized the ground's pristine white cover. "Remember, it snowed last night."

"Not enough to completely cover furrows made by

a wolf who was running confused and scared, not to mention dragging chains and grapples.''

A chill shot through her. ''C'mon, Donovan. What are you saying?'' she asked uneasily. ''That a leghold trap up and walked away?''

''Just like the congressman's car.''

HAVING PULLED UP a chair and footstool near the Franklin stove, Laurel was warming her stockinged feet, sipping at her coffee and doing some hard thinking. Donovan had used the radio to check on his father through someone in the sheriff's office. *Condition holding.* Now he seemed to be thinking, as well, pacing the length of the room and ignoring the coffee mug in his hand.

''It all has to be connected,'' he muttered, tone low and acrid. *''Everything.''*

Why did she get the feeling he was talking about a whole lot more than a disappearing car and wolf trap?

''Define *everything,*'' she said.

He started, as if he'd forgotten her presence. ''Things have been going wrong for months now. Livestock being killed out of territory when there's a surplus of deer. A wolf disappearing...now a trap. Blood I sent to the lab to be analyzed never arriving. And an outsider has invaded this land several times.''

He stopped in front of a window and stared out into the fast-falling darkness as if he could spot his enemy.

Despite sitting so close to the stove, Laurel felt more and more chilled. Anyone else might think Donovan paranoid, especially after observing his strange behavior when they'd arrived back at the cabin nearly an hour ago.

He'd gone on alert.

She couldn't describe it any other way. He'd had that frozen-sentient demeanor she'd seen in her own dogs when they picked up a disturbing scent or sound. For a heart-pounding moment, Donovan had stood on the front stoop…listening…watching…sniffing the air.…

Like a wild animal protective of his territory.

In the end, he'd come inside without saying a word. Flesh crawling, she'd followed.

"I've sensed him…and found his tracks," he went on. "I mistakenly imagined a hunter not satisfied with public lands. But now I know…an intruder spying…waiting for an opening…"

Considering how she'd gotten to be temporary roommates with the man, she figured he was on to something.

"A man posing as you, showing me professional journals with articles written by you about wolf behavior…" she mused "…maybe someone who wants to bring the recovery program to a screeching halt…and who happened to have a run-in with your father to boot."

They connected for a moment, and Laurel could sense they were on the same wavelength. If all the things they were talking about were connected, then she hadn't simply been fooled—she had been used. But to what end? What part had she been assigned to play in the unfolding drama? How would her marrying the fake Donovan have served his purpose?

No way could the imposter have known she would involve Raymond. Right?

Amber eyes burning into her, Donovan said, "Tell me how you met him. What he said to you. How he acted. Anything that might give me a clue."

While Laurel still didn't relish rehashing the events that led her to this point, she knew it to be a necessary evil. Still, she couldn't help but be self-conscious under the close scrutiny of someone as judgmental as Donovan. He would probably condemn her for being so gullible. A swig of coffee gave her courage.

"Saturday night at the wolf ecology workshop," she began, "we were out in the woods, broken into several groups for a howling. Afterward, when we were heading back to the center, I was straggling behind a little. One minute I was alone, the next he was just there beside me."

"And that's the first time you saw him?"

"Actually, I'd noticed him at the back of the room during one of the lectures that afternoon. He kept to himself, then disappeared before we broke for dinner. I asked him about it. He said he wasn't officially part of the workshop. He introduced himself as Donovan Wilde and claimed he was a field biologist studying wolves." She tried distancing herself from the hurt, but she wasn't good at burying her emotions. "I had no reason to disbelieve him."

"If he wasn't part of the workshop, how did he justify his being there?"

"He claimed that he'd dropped by to check in with a friend who was part of the staff."

"Did he mention a name?"

She shook her head. "And there were more than a

half-dozen WRIN volunteers present. Of course, that's assuming he was telling the truth about knowing someone. I never saw him talking to anyone else.''

Which should have been her first clue that something was wrong, Laurel thought. Had she been purposely blind or merely naive? She couldn't help ragging on herself. City smart, she wouldn't give a guy who tried picking her up on the streets of Chicago the time of day, no less believe his line. But put her in the middle of the woods and, rather than being honed, her sense of self-preservation was shot to hell.

She sipped at her lukewarm coffee.

Repositioning the other armchair close to hers, Donovan threw himself into it. ''What happened after this guy introduced himself?''

''When we arrived back at the center, he asked if I'd like to go into town for a beer. It was still early. Barely ten. I figured...what could be the harm.''

She never imagined the chain of events her accepting a simple beer would set in motion—that she'd be responsible for a man being injured. Or worse.

''So, you spent the night with him?''

Was that his judgmental face? Laurel wondered, biting her tongue to keep herself from snapping at him.

Instead, she said, ''I spent a couple of hours with the man,'' and emphasized, *''talking,''* so that he would be clear on how she'd been lulled into trusting a stranger.

''About?''

Maybe he hadn't meant anything by the question, after all. ''Come to think of it,'' a relieved Laurel

said, "the conversation was pretty one-sided. He
wanted to know all about me...didn't talk much about
himself. Not then, anyway. He walked me to my car
and said he'd call. I took the beer at face value and
figured he was being polite."

How could she have suspected he'd had some dark
agenda?

"How long did it take him to follow up?"

"A couple of days. He said he was coming into
Chicago to visit family and wanted to see me."

"When was that?"

"Mid-December. At first, I figured he was around
a lot during the holidays because of family. Then January rolled around, and he still made it into the city
for a couple of days here and there. He made it clear
that he was coming back and forth just to see me."

"Why you?" he murmured, echoing his mother.

Thinking of her rescuer theory, Laurel was reluctant to share something so personal with this hard-
edged man. "I suppose he figured I was gullible."

"Or he knew you lived in Chicago..."

As had Raymond McKenna and Donovan's siblings, she silently finished. "You think he was trying
to hook me up with your family?"

"Something to consider," he said thoughtfully.
"Did you ever visit him here in Wisconsin?"

"I was never invited. He talked about being too
busy with the wolves to pay me proper attention....
But I should have known something was wrong when
he couldn't give me a telephone number where I
could reach him." Then it hit her. "Although *you*
don't have a phone. Why not?"

"Out here?"

"Cell phones work practically anywhere."

"An abominable thought," he said before switching the conversation back to the imposter. "What did this guy look like?"

Abominable because he didn't consider cell phones appropriate with nature? Or because it would make him too accessible to the outside world?

Noting his impatient expression, she said, "His description would fit you, at least superficially. Tall, medium build, dark hair, light eyes—though his were gray. He didn't really look like you, though. Fair-skinned, medium nose, pointed lips, small cleft in his chin."

Her Donovan had been far more handsome, if in a conventional sense. But Laurel was beginning to think she preferred the real Donovan's more exotic looks. The way his edgy features reflected his inner strength, as well as the deep-seated anger he'd never dealt with.

At the moment, he was as intense as she'd ever seen him. Brow furrowed. Mouth set in a grim line. Amber eyes burning—not at her this time, but turned inward.

Taking the advantage, Laurel stared, soon realizing something weird was happening to her. Pulse accelerating. Breath shortening. Chest tightening.

She set the mug of coffee away from her. Either she'd had too much caffeine…or too much of him. She'd prefer the first option.

No way was she ready to admit an attraction to another man. Not when she couldn't trust her own judgment.

"It's not coming," he finally said.

"What?"

"That description you gave. I can't attach a name to it. I don't even know the guy."

"Sleep on it. Maybe it'll come to you."

"There's nothing wrong with my memory," Donovan countered. "If I had seen him, I would remember."

Deflated, fearing they were on the wrong track, Laurel said, "Then this doesn't make sense—a man you don't even know pretending to be you."

"Maybe he owed someone else a favor. Or money. Or maybe he was *hired* to do some mischief."

Could that be what had been troubling the fake Donovan? Laurel wondered. Doing someone else's bidding for whatever reason...and not liking it?

Perhaps getting to know her had made the imposter back out of the plan. His conscience catching up to him would explain the vanishing act.

Oddly enough, the thought made her feel a little better. A bit less foolish for getting involved with a man who'd set out to trick her. Even now she couldn't think of him without the hurt that came of caring. She could hardly believe it, but other than being angry and depressed, her feelings hadn't done a one-eighty. They'd merely grown more complex.

Fearing that unless she made an effort she'd be swamped by tears, Laurel forced herself back to her brainstorming session with the real Donovan.

"Who might want to see the recovery program ruined?" she asked. "Other than Ham Gault."

"Another hunter...a farmer who lost livestock...someone who wants this land?"

The last startled her. "The land? Doesn't it belong to the state?"

He shook his head. "It's being held in trust. The late owner, Matthew Lemley, was dedicated to the wolf recovery program. He made great contributions to WRIN, even headed the organization for a few years."

WRIN—Wolf Recovery Information Network— the organization that had sponsored the workshop.

Donovan continued, "Lemley built this cabin, moved from town to be closer to Mother Nature. In the meantime, the wolves' numbers were increasing. They were spreading out. Coming closer. Lemley always hoped a couple of dispersers would move in with him."

"Lone wolves?" she mused. *Like Donovan?*

"No such animal, at least not by choice. Dispersers are wolves who aren't content to remain part of a pack where they have no authority. Unless they want to be a bider—wait for the opportunity to move up to alpha status—they leave. They look for their own territory and a mate from a different pack. It's nature's way of renewing those gene pools so the wolves aren't all inbred."

Laurel remembered the basics from the workshop. No wolves bred but the alpha male and female. The rest of the pack usually consisted mostly of yearlings, in addition to the new pups. Once in a while an older wolf or one from another pack would hang around for years waiting for a chance to be top wolf. And then there was the bottom wolf. The omega. The screwup. Picked on. The last to feed.

At the moment, she was feeling a bit omegaish herself.

She said, "Mr. Lemley must have been thrilled when his dream finally came true."

"Mere months too late. He died before he could see it happen." Donovan's expression relayed his regret. "He left this property in trust as an animal preserve, at least until the year 2000. He specified that, if no wolves had made the land part of their territory by then, it would revert to his estate."

"But the wolves *are* here now."

"True. But if they were to be driven off because of the danger to humans…"

She got his point. "So, who benefits?"

"Lemley's niece. After she was widowed, Karen Tobin lived with and did for her uncle for several years. That's when he was still in town, of course. But eventually she decided she missed her son too much and moved to Sheboygan to be near him. I was in Idaho at the time, so this is all hearsay. And I only met the woman once—late last fall."

"But you must have formed an opinion." She could see it in the disapproving pull of his mouth.

"Lemley's niece wasn't pleased with the trust and didn't make any bones about saying so. She also threatened to break it—said she and her son wouldn't be cheated. But Lemley was of sound mind and had a good lawyer, so I didn't take her too seriously. So far, she hasn't succeeded."

"That's legally," Laurel mused. "Do you think she's capable of working *outside* the system?"

"Maybe. It's certainly something to keep in mind."

DONOVAN STARED DOWN at the open journal in his lap. Every night, he faithfully recorded his observations of the day, anything having to do with the wolves. This was the heart of his research, the basis for the papers that he wrote for professional journals.

But tonight the words wouldn't flow.

Karen Tobin wouldn't get out of his head.

He closed the journal and set it on the coffee table.

The thought that *she* might be behind the strange happenings that put the wolves in a bad light had never occurred to him before. And why should it now? He couldn't imagine her creeping around the property and spying on him, although she might try to bulldoze her way in.

The son David, however, remained a question mark.

Judging by Lemley, who'd been close to eighty when he'd died, his niece was probably in her fifties, which meant her son could be in his late twenties or early thirties. *His own age or close enough.* And Sheboygan was only a two and a half hour drive from Chicago, easy enough for someone to get back and forth on a regular basis....

But was David Tobin clever enough and devious enough to get away with pretending to be a wolfman?

And to fool Laurel into believing it?

Even if wolves weren't his thing, Tobin must have picked up some knowledge from his grandfather.

And Laurel Newkirk was too naive, too trusting, too openhearted for her own good. Obviously, no one had ever taught her to think with her head.

Not that anyone had taught him, either. He'd learned the hard way at the age of eight. What a rude awakening that had been.

The sound of the shower running caught him, sparked his imagination, whet appetites that he'd been ignoring for more months than he cared to count. He could almost envision the rivulets of soapy water fingering her flesh....

Laurel.

He'd had his share of women, but he'd kept his relationships casual and short-lived. His work was his life and he hadn't met the woman who both attracted him and understood what he was about. The last one actually had the gall to say that she didn't have the patience to compete with those *disgusting creatures* of his. That had been it for him.

And he hadn't met anyone who'd stirred his blood since leaving Idaho the year before.

Until now...

But there was no percentage in it, Donovan told himself. Laurel needed someone stable. Down to earth. Committed.

And he needed...

Donovan didn't know what he needed, other than a soft body to fill his arms and nights. Laurel wouldn't even be that. She'd be gone tomorrow. Besides, she was too angular for his taste. All long limbs and a decided lack of curves.

But when the bathroom door opened a few minutes later, and she stepped into the room wearing nothing but the T-shirt and socks he'd lent her as night wear, his body told him otherwise. While loose enough to bag around her nearly to her knees, the white cotton also clung in places to her damp skin. Not that she seemed to realize it.

Raising her arms, she unwrapped the towel from

her wet hair…and in the process, stretched the thin material across her breasts.

Her nipples puckered against the damp cotton.

"You're sure about the sleeping arrangements?" she asked.

Unable to rip his gaze from the intriguing if modest sight, he muttered, "Positive."

Liar. His groin insisted that he really wanted to be sleeping in his bed, all right. *With her.*

"That couch would fit me better than you," she continued, provocatively rubbing wet strands of her hair with the terry cloth.

"We've been over this," he snapped, then felt a bit reprehensible when he sensed her withdrawal.

Expression tight, she backed up. "Fine." Then she whirled around and into his bedroom. As she retreated, she gave him a pulse-pounding view of her derriere.

Fine didn't quite cover it.

Thank God she disappeared from sight, giving him a chance to cool down.

But a moment later, when, voice sounding odd, she called out, "Donovan, is this some kind of joke?" he shot out of the chair like an arrow released from a deer hunter's bow.

He reached the doorway to see her bending over the bed, the center of which was decorated with a piece of the stink bait he used to trap wolves. Hardly having time to consider the situation, he acted on instinct.

"No!" he yelled, flying from the doorway even as her fingers were about to close around the bait. He tackled her, jerking back her arm.

A metallic *thwunk* accompanied her cry of, "What's wrong with you?"

They rolled together over the mattress, coming to a stop at the foot of the bed.

He landed on top.

Her expression at once angry and confused, Laurel gasped and ineffectually tried to push him off. "If you wanted the damn bed," she snarled, "why didn't you just say so?"

He found himself by saying, "Actions speak louder than words."

Startling himself by making a joke.

Up close and personal, Laurel wasn't wanting in any department. She'd fill his arms just fine. Long legs tangling with his as she squirmed beneath him, she set off a five-alarm fire that Donovan knew only one way to quench.

But this wasn't the time, not when the intruder had taken things a step further, had invaded his space while they'd been checking the traps. For all he knew, the bastard could be lurking...watching even now...waiting to see if his warped plot had come to fruition.

He fought his natural urges so that he could focus on the situation.

And release a breathless Laurel.

"Mind telling me what that was about?" she murmured as she grabbed the T-shirt in a white-knuckled hand, loosening it from her still-damp body.

"We had an uninvited guest."

One look at her soft expression, one glance from eyes hiding banked fires, and Donovan knew that Laurel had been turned on as much as he had. Obviously trying to hide the fact, she shifted her gaze away from him and to the bed.

Knowing what he'd find, he threw back the spread to reveal the mystery of the missing wolf trap.

Chapter Six

Laurel trembled inside. The reaction spread and she began to shake. A sudden chill stole through her, chasing away the heat of her recent body contact with Donovan. She wrapped her arms around her midsection, as though that could warm her. But the cold wasn't coming from the room—it was coming from deep inside. She hadn't been so frightened since she'd realized her grandmother was dying six years ago.

"Omigod...he meant to hurt me, didn't he?"

"Whoever set this trap couldn't have known I wouldn't be sleeping in my own bed," Donovan assured her. "That was meant for me, not you."

She stared at the sprung leghold trap. How cleverly it had been concealed. The perpetrator had dug a hole out of the mattress large enough to sink the device. Had Donovan not acted so quickly, the steel jaws would have clamped onto her arm instead of thin air.

She knew the trap was meant to be harmless to wolves—while it would surround the animal's thin leg, the opening was made too narrow to pull the much larger paw free. That way, the device would hinder the wolf from loping off, without actually doing any damage.

A human arm was far thicker than a wolf's leg, however. Laurel visually measured the opening against her own arm and found it lacking.

"That th-thing would have b-broken a bone." Even her voice was shaky now. "Th-thanks."

"You're not going to start crying on me, are you?"

Though she felt the sting at the back of her lids, Laurel shook her head. "N-no, of course not."

"Because I hate it when women cry."

"M-me, t-too," she said, twin tears escaping despite her best efforts to contain them.

"Nothing attractive about a sobbing woman with red eyes and a runny nose."

She nodded in agreement and unsuccessfully tried to choke back a sob.

"Oh, hell!"

Grabbing her upper arm, Donovan whipped her against his chest so fast that Laurel didn't have the presence of mind to stop him...even if stopping him had been what she wanted.

He was offering her a broad set of shoulders to lean on. Sniffling, Laurel snaked her arms around his waist, and in that moment, felt more for Donovan than she'd ever felt for the man who'd stolen his identity. Shocked, she wondered how that could be. She hardly knew this wolfman, and yet she clung to him like a lifeline.

The urge to cry quickly abated.

The shaking stopped.

And a confused Laurel began feeling other things,

more intimate things, even as she had for those few
seconds when he'd pressed her into the mattress.

"Better?" he asked, voice gruff.

She nodded and murmured, "Mm-hmm."

Aware of his hand stroking her back, Laurel closed
her eyes and concentrated on sheer physical sensation.
For a moment, she lost herself in the soothing touch
of his palm, in the strength of his fingers, in the hard
heat of his body pressed up against hers.

Just as Donovan must be losing himself in her, if
his repeated, "Oh, hell!"—though softer this time—
was any indication.

So quickly that she didn't have time to protest, he
bent his head and possessed her mouth in a deep,
searching kiss that left her instantly weak-kneed.

And, as if it were the most natural response in the
world, she kissed him back.

Mouths melded...tongues touched...bodies butted
against each other.

A perfect fit.

No other way to describe it, she thought hazily,
mentally surrendering to the inevitable. No man had
ever had such an instantaneous and total affect on her,
no matter the emotion. Whether fear or anger or desire, he had her every time.

His hands cradled her head as he angled his
mouth...as if he wanted all of her.

Her fingers tangled through his long hair, loosened
from the leather tie...as if she couldn't get enough of
him.

She yearned...burned...ached.

All the things previously denied her in relationships
with other men.

Donovan trailed one hand down her spine, leaving in its wake flesh that quaked for more of his touch. And when he cradled her bottom, she couldn't help herself. With a sigh, she rocked her hips into his, her center brushing his.

And then she was abruptly set aside.

Her eyes jerked open. Laurel blinked, confused, reluctant to face reality.

Realizing the material of his pullover was fisted in her hands, she let go, murmuring, "Oh...sorry," though she wasn't really.

She'd needed comforting and Donovan's arms had done the job. They'd felt so right around her. His lips had done an even better job, drawing her to the brink before launching her toward free fall. He'd offered exactly what she'd needed, Laurel told herself.

For the moment.

She was reluctant to analyze further or to think ahead. Not now. Not with Donovan's gaze burning into her, making her self-conscious.

Making her insides flame with a hunger she didn't understand.

He broke the spell, saying, "I'd better take a look around outside."

Though the growl was back in his voice, she ignored it and said, "I'll go with you."

Her lips felt strange. Swollen and sensual and tight and angry. Her breasts did, too. And the secret place between her thighs. His effect on her was too powerful to deny.

"You'd slow me down," Donovan said as he headed for the front door. "Besides, you just got out of the shower. I won't be playing nursemaid to your pneumonia.''

Her irritation with him escalating, she followed. ''As if I would want you to!''

How could he kiss her as he had, then pretend nothing had happened between them?

''Stay put,'' he ordered, donning his deerskin jacket.

''Stop ordering me around!''

Despite the intimacy shared only a moment ago, he gave her a look meant to intimidate.

Laurel's pulse jagged, but this time it wasn't because of him. At least not due to a reaction *to* him.

Somehow she understood what he wasn't saying, as if he could speak to her without words.

And try as she might, she couldn't totally repress her growing fear that came with understanding. She watched in silence as Donovan slipped his hands into gloves and threw on his headgear, then fastened the leather belt securing a sheathed knife to his waist.

A knife.

A weapon!

While he'd worn it before, she'd thought of the knife as a tool he used in his work, but now it seemed to have a more ominous intent.

Donovan's amber eyes met hers briefly, as he said, ''Get dressed...just in case.''

In case what?

Before she could find the voice to ask, he left the cabin, flashlight in hand.

Already feeling too alone, Laurel told herself there was no reason to panic. He hadn't taken his snowshoes, so he couldn't be going far. As per his order, she started pulling on clothes—thermal underwear, jeans and sweatshirt—while dancing from window to window to keep an eye on him.

The night was bright, and she watched Donovan check the ground for tracks. He obviously wasn't finding anything that concerned him. Only when he was directly outside the back door—she was hopping on one foot to pull her boot on the other—did he stoop to get a closer view. Then he stood and shone his flashlight along the ground in a slow if direct sweep away from the cabin. As she knew he would, he followed the beam of light toward the trees.

Laurel's apprehension began escalating when he didn't seem inclined to stop. Fearing he would soon be out of sight, she told herself to stay calm, but her body wasn't cooperating. Her heart thudded against her ribs, and her chest tightened. The air in the cabin suddenly threatened to suffocate her.

What if something happened to Donovan...and her without a clue?

He could be lying out there, helpless, while she'd be a sitting duck.

Not if she could help it!

Hesitating only a heartbeat, Laurel ran for the jacket he'd lent her and threw it on. Even as she pulled the hood over her still-damp hair, she flew out the back door. She focused on the path he'd taken.

No trace of Donovan but his tracks.

The night grabbed her with icy fingers, but Laurel ignored the cold. Fear alone was enough to keep her warm. She raced along the path Donovan had taken, wishing only that she had some form of protection—

though she abhorred the thought of carrying a weapon.

"Big threat I'd be," she mumbled, as usual taking comfort in her own voice. "I can see it now. Me holding a gun—'Get your hands up, buddy'—him having a good laugh because he can tell I would never use the damn thing!"

The moon was nearly full and was thus bright enough to light the way. She kept her gaze moving, searching, seeking out danger. But the land lay around her in pristine innocence, as if nothing sinister could ever mar it.

But something sinister had nearly touched *her,* Laurel thought. Had it not been for Donovan's quick thinking... Thrashing through a stand of pine trees, she reached another clearing and a small incline.

Donovan!

Anxiety abating as quickly as it had gripped her, Laurel stopped dead in her tracks. She suddenly felt weak-kneed and foolish.

For, as hardy as she'd ever seen him, Donovan stood on the rise, face tilted toward the moon, cupped hands around his mouth. She'd never been so glad to see anyone in her life!

"Awroo-oo-oo-oo-oo..."

His primal howl sent a shudder through her.

Lowering his arms, he balled fists on his hips and stared out into the night as if looking for something. The villain who'd invaded his home? Laurel almost called out to him, but instinct stopped her. Not that she was trying to hide her presence. A sense of something about to happen—something that had nothing to do with the leghold trap—rooted her to where she stood.

"Ruu-aww-aww-woo-oo-oo-oo…"

A response. Flesh crawled along her spine at the mournful wail. She waited for the others to follow.

None came.

Donovan ripped off an answering call. *"Ow-ow-ow-wwww…"*

After which the night grew eerily still.

Laurel strained to hear over the sound of her own labored breathing. She concentrated hard, eventually imagining she heard the quick, precise movements of an animal.…

To her left, a silhouette slid from the shadows. A dark, shaggy body topping spindly legs and large paws. A bigger animal than her largest dog, he had to weigh close to a hundred pounds, a lot even for a wolf.

She could hardly believe it. Most people—even trackers—never actually got to see a wolf in the wild. She shot a glance toward Donovan.

He didn't seem to be the least bit impressed…or wary.

As a matter of fact, he was acting as if this were the most natural thing in the world.

As if he'd done this before, dozens of times.

Her pulse raced with excitement at the scene unfolding before her even as she remembered the speculation between the grizzled men in the café…how she'd silently defended Donovan…denied that any human could have control over a wild creature.

Donovan hunkered down to the level of the black wolf, who, in return, lowered his body, ducked his

head and flattened his ears as he shot forward and up
the incline, straight toward the human. He whined
before lifting his nose to Donovan's face and giving
the wolfman's lips a lick in greeting.

Active submission.

Laurel's eye widened and she continued watching,
mesmerized, in silent awe. She'd seen this behavior
with dogs and their masters, including her own.

But a wild wolf recognizing a human as its alpha?
The concept stole her breath away.

She backed off, choosing to leave without his ever
knowing she'd witnessed what he'd surely meant to
keep private.

"YOU'RE DOING the right thing, Donovan," Laurel
murmured the next morning.

She slipped by him and followed his mother into
the lobby of Nicolet General Hospital. They'd passed
a couple of reporter types, who luckily didn't seem
aware of the new arrivals.

Donovan entered last and with great reluctance.
He'd been done with the place until his mother had
insisted he escort her there. He'd known she was ma-
nipulating him and he'd let her, maybe because he'd
recognized the expression deep in her eyes as one of
panic. Even now, she wasn't herself—not the same
steady woman he'd depended on all his life. Now he
had to be there for her.

Pale and unusually silent during the entire drive to
the hospital, she'd seemed vulnerable—a description
that had never fit her well before—as if Raymond
McKenna meant more to her than just being the father
to her son.

To top off his morning, Laurel had had the temerity to tag along after announcing she would not be mentally or physically coerced onto that bus out of town. How had he guessed he wouldn't rid himself of the city woman so easily?

How badly he really wanted her gone was another question—a bag of worms he was not willing to open. No matter that he tried, he couldn't put that kiss out of his head. Not even the bitter cold of the night before had done the trick.

He only knew that when he'd come back into the cabin and found her on the couch pretending to be asleep, he'd wanted to take her in his arms and hold her all night. Instead, he'd grabbed a sleeping bag and had stretched out on the floor between her and the stove.

The bed with its gouged-out mattress and lingering, if faint, scent of stink bait had been truly unappealing. He'd consider locking his doors from now on if he didn't know locks wouldn't stop a man with a mission.

As the tracks had confirmed...

He'd had hours to think seriously about the trap that had been set in his bed. Surely the intruder hadn't figured he'd be green enough to pick up the bait without first checking things out. He'd come to the conclusion that the incident had been more of a warning—perhaps a challenge—than an actual threat.

Arriving at the reception desk brought Donovan back to the present. He introduced himself and asked for the location of the intensive care unit.

"Dr. Graves would like to speak to you before you

see Congressman McKenna,'' the receptionist said instead.

"Why?'' his mother asked anxiously. "Has something happened?''

"I wouldn't know, ma'am. I'm just passing on the message.''

"There shouldn't be any problem with our going on to the ICU waiting room,'' Laurel said. "Right? Mr. Wilde's sister is probably there now. Alone.''

"Oh, of course. And I'll tell Dr. Graves you've arrived as soon as he's free.''

The receptionist gave them directions to the intensive care unit, located on the second floor.

Once in the elevator, Donovan could see that his mother was becoming more agitated. He took her hand and squeezed it.

And as they walked down the second-floor corridor, she whispered, "You don't think Aileen will object to my seeing your father, do you?''

"It would be out of character for her,'' he said, his own discomfort growing.

Aileen was the only McKenna who'd tried treating him like one. She was all right, but he'd never allowed himself to get too attached. After all, Aileen was LaVerne's daughter—LaVerne being the woman his father had married even while his mother had been pregnant with him. As far as he was concerned, getting close to his half sister would be like slapping his mother in the face.

When they entered the waiting area outside the intensive care unit, the first thing Donovan saw was Aileen curled up in a love seat, bright raspberry coat thrown over her like a blanket. But as if sensing their presence, she sat up abruptly, strawberry-blond hair tousled around her sweet face.

A face that crumpled when she saw him. "Donovan!" She raced for him and threw herself into his arms, not giving him a chance to escape her desperate hug. "You came," she sobbed. "I knew you would! I told Skelly…" She took a big breath and looked up at him through wet eyes. "You heard what happened, right?"

His heart stilled and he went cold inside—his first thought being that their father had died during the night. "What?" he asked, his gripping her too hard the only trace of the emotion that suddenly pierced him.

Eyes widening in understanding, she shook her head. "Donovan, no. He's all right now. But earlier this morning, the drainage tube they'd placed through his skull to release excess fluids somehow got knocked out. Thank God the ICU nurse caught the problem before the pressure built up and there was any real damage."

As Donovan took a relieved breath, his mother murmured, "I have to see him."

"Don't worry, Mom, you will." He let go of Aileen. "Did they say how it happened?"

She shrugged. "An accident."

No doubt what Dr. Graves wanted to discuss with him, perhaps to circumvent the threat of a malpractice suit. Not that *he* would be the one to make such a decision.…

"So many people go in and out of ICU to check on the patients," Laurel said with the ring of authority. "Nurses, respiratory therapists, lab technicians, doctors. Any one of them could have disturbed the drain without realizing it.''

Donovan determined Laurel looked about as stressed as he felt. He remembered her saying she'd lost the people she'd loved and wondered exactly how personally involved she'd been in their tragedies. From the knowledge she displayed—from her very nature—he'd guess quite a bit. A lot to take on for someone so young. Undoubtedly being here was nearly as difficult for her as it was for him…if in a different way.

And noting how exhausted Aileen appeared, Donovan wondered if she'd left the intensive-care area since she'd arrived.

Where the hell was Skelly, anyway? How ironic that his father's favorite couldn't be bothered to show his face where it was needed. And after all the praise the old man had heaped on him, too. He'd used every chance he'd had to praise Skelly, making certain Donovan knew who counted and who didn't. So, why wasn't Mr. Wonderful here, not only for his father, but for his sister?

''When was the last time you ate?'' he asked Aileen.

''I don't know. A nurse gave me some orange juice—''

''Food.''

She shrugged.

What? She didn't know? Didn't care? Maybe both? At this rate, she might as well check *herself* in.

''Laurel,'' he said, thinking of a way to distract them both for a while, ''would you mind keeping Aileen company while she gets some breakfast?''

"I really shouldn't leave," his sister protested. "What if something—"

"I'm here, and you need a break. And I'll know to find you in the cafeteria."

"C'mon," Laurel said, taking the ball and running with it. "I could use a good cup of coffee myself. That stuff your brother makes is mud."

Donovan raised an eyebrow as Laurel placed an arm around Aileen's shoulders and led her back toward the elevator. Earlier, she'd slugged down half a pot of that mud.

Then he turned to make certain his mother was all right, only to find she'd done a disappearing act on him. He waited a moment before rounding the corner to the nurses' station, a hub in the center of half a dozen patient rooms.

"I'm Congressman McKenna's son," he told the only nurse behind the counter. "My mother—"

A buzzer went off.

"Can it wait a minute?" the harried-sounding woman asked.

"Sure."

She hurried to the room on the far left.

He glanced at the chart hanging adjacent to the door on the right. Samuel Pearson. The next chart read Wayne Holt. Still no nurse by the time he arrived at one of the center doors. He didn't have to check the paperwork—he heard his mother's voice.

"...can't stand seeing you like this..."

Donovan stepped into the room but didn't announce himself.

"I remember what a fine figure of a man you were," she murmured, her tone enticing in a nonsexual manner. "Straight from the old sod. Proud. Handsome. Strong."

She sat by his father's bed, her fingers lightly touching his free hand. The other was taped to a board, an IV protruding from the back, and one of his fingertips was cuffed for vitals.

"So strong, especially in your convictions."

From beneath his hospital gown, lines from EKG electrodes ran to a monitor. And his face was slightly distorted by his oxygen nasal cannula. The all-important drain seemed to be in place.

"I know it couldn't have worked between us, Raymond, but I couldn't…"

His mother's emotion-filled voice trailed off. Damn! He'd thought she'd gotten over his father's duplicity, but obviously the fact that he'd abandoned her—abandoned *them*—was still a source of pain. Donovan stepped closer to comfort her and saw his father's eyes open.

"Raymond? Raymond, can you hear me? Say something," his mother pleaded.

Slowly, without recognition of any kind, his eyes slid closed once more.

And Donovan put a hand on his mother's shoulder. "Mom?"

She looked up at him and smiled. "Did you see? He opened his eyes. He's coming back to us!"

"Maybe."

At that moment, Donovan realized his mother felt more than pain for the man who'd betrayed her. For God's sake, no matter what he'd done to her, no matter how badly he'd betrayed her, she still loved Raymond McKenna!

"Your father's going to be all right, Donny," she was saying, a catch in her words. "He recognized my voice."

"It's something to discuss with Dr. Graves," he said, not committing himself one way or the other. "We'd better go look for him."

Where his father was concerned, Donovan refused to get his hopes up.

The old man always had had a way of disappointing him.

"WHY ARE YOU still here?" Aileen asked Laurel as she picked at her food. "Not that I'm objecting. I was just wondering. You do have a life, right? And a job?"

"Yeah, I have a job. I also have personal days."

And sick days. And vacation days. Too responsible for her own good—as she'd been told more than once by co-workers—she rarely took the time due her. No doubt they'd be shocked when they learned she'd called in to take a few.

"You're feeling guilty, Laurel, but you shouldn't. What happened to our father wasn't your fault."

Laurel wondered how much the other woman knew about what was going on. Probably nothing more than the fact that her father had been attacked, and chances were it was by a wolf. She didn't feel it was up to her to inform Aileen otherwise. And what could she say, really, that had any basis in fact, other than someone had it out for the recovery program?

Remembering the trap in the bed, she suddenly realized Aileen was waiting for a response. Laurel gave her one that came from the heart.

"I *am* to blame. If I hadn't shown up on your father's doorstep with my fantastical story—"

Aileen cut in. "Are you saying that you lied?"

"No! Just...I shouldn't have been so gullible in the first place."

She felt a little odd discussing her naiveté with so many strangers around to overhear. But, as was true of every other hospital cafeteria she'd been in, the people around her were too involved with their own problems to be concerned with hers.

A man and woman, hands clasped.

A young mother with a tear-streaked face tending to her two young children.

An elderly man, back bowed, staring into his mug. For a moment, she empathized with him. How many times had she sat alone waiting for word on her grandmother? Her throat closed up and her eyes began to sting....

"Trust is a virtue not many people have," Aileen was saying. "Take Donovan. He could use a dose."

Only one of his shortcomings, Laurel thought grumpily. But all she said was, "He thinks he has good reasons to be distrustful."

"He does," Aileen admitted. "It was tough on him, you know, being the odd one out. And Skelly didn't help." She shook her head and muttered, "What a cretin he could be!"

"You and Skelly don't get along, either?"

The other woman appeared taken aback at the idea. "There isn't anything Skelly wouldn't do for me," she protested. "Or I for him. But there have been times I've wanted to shoot him, too. That's the way real life is between siblings. Even half siblings. Ups and downs. Fighting, then sticking up for each other. Donovan just…didn't get it.''

"You really care for him."

"Are you kidding? I used to worship him. Whenever Dad brought Donovan for a visit, I followed him around and made a general nuisance of myself. He was so independent, so competent, so tough.''

"Independent and tough describe him," Laurel said with a sigh.

After giving in to a tender moment, a connection she wanted to explore further, Donovan was acting like nothing at all had happened between them.

"But he could also be amazingly gentle," his sister added. ''After he fixed my cat's paw when she hurt it in the garden, he was my hero. No one could say any wrong about him, not even Skelly. I was five and I announced I was going to marry him to anyone who'd listen. Dad laughed and told me that would be the same as my marrying Skelly because they were both equally my brothers. I was heartbroken…at least for a couple of weeks.''

Laurel laughed, but she didn't miss the implication that the congressman had put Donovan in the same category as his older son.

Surely Donovan hadn't been too pigheaded to admit as much, she murmured, "I doubt he has a clue.''

"Donovan never had a clue. He didn't want to. He was determined not to like us from the first. I see that now, in retrospect. It never occurred to me as a child that anyone should dislike me, so I ignored his attitude. Eventually, Donovan grew to…well, like me, I guess…if grudgingly.''

"What about Skelly?''

"He was a boy...and a typical male. Competitive. Belligerent. He was always trying to one-up Donovan."

"He's a grown man now."

"Well...in most ways."

They laughed together and Laurel decided she liked Donovan's sister. A lot.

"Skelly should arrive somewhere around noon," Aileen said. "I called right after this morning's alarm. Too bad he and Donovan can't find some common ground."

"They already *have* common ground. Your father."

Though Laurel wasn't certain that Donovan would have stepped one foot back in this hospital if not for his mother.

"You have a point. Maybe they can find each other in a time of crisis. Maybe this family can still be healed. If only for that, Dad *has* to recover," Aileen said, obviously trying to convince herself. "It just can't be too late."

Chapter Seven

A Donovan-Skelly reunion would have to wait for another day. They left the hospital before the congressman's firstborn arrived, purposely to avoid him, Laurel expected, though the excuse Donovan used was work. Both his and his mother's. He had traps to check and she a café to open for the lunch crowd.

By now the reporters had caught on to Donovan's identity, however, and surrounded the three of them as they made their way to the Tracker.

Followed by a newscam, a woman holding a microphone was the first to intercept him. "Mr. Wilde, can you update us on Congressman McKenna's condition?"

Donovan refused to so much as recognize her presence.

A man danced backward as he asked, "How do you feel about one of your wolves attacking your father?"

"And *you*, ma'am," another said, aiming his question at Veronica, "how do *you* fit into this picture?"

Glaring at the man, Donovan pushed him out of

the way. Laurel wouldn't have blamed him if he'd done worse.

"Hey! Should I quote you on that?" the angry reporter demanded.

Wrapping a protective arm around his mother until they reached the Tracker, Donovan helped her into the front passenger seat. Then he gave Laurel a hand into the rear.

"Mr. Wilde, wait!" called the television newswoman.

"I need a sound bite, please!" someone else yelled. "From anyone!"

A picturesque figure, a fearless Trapper Dan plowed through them all, unhesitating even as cameras flashed and the newscam light went on. Sliding behind the wheel, he started up the Tracker and drove it out as though the pavement were clear of people. As, indeed, it shortly was, Laurel noted. Reporters scattered in every direction to get out of his way.

"Vultures."

Donovan's low growl was the only thing said until they were halfway to Iron Lake.

"I'm going back to the hospital tomorrow," Veronica suddenly announced. "Raymond needs me."

"He has his children to take care of him," Donovan told her, as if he weren't one of them.

His mother glared at him, but he didn't break. Tension radiated all the way into the back seat. Laurel figured keeping her mouth shut was her smartest option.

Finally, Veronica said, "He responded to my voice."

"You don't know that."

"Dr. Graves said it was quite possible. And that his opening his eyes when I was speaking to him was a positive sign."

"So, he'll open them again."

"I'll make sure of it," his mother vowed. "I'll go every day until he's himself."

Laurel had been there when Dr. Graves suggested that coma patients rarely snapped back all at once. And if, indeed, the congressman was coming around, then hearing a familiar voice would help him focus. Still, he would come back in stages, and it might possibly take several days before he was able to make the connection between the voice and the person speaking.

"Do you really think you're the only one who can save him?" Donovan demanded.

"No. *You* could help. Think of how much it would mean to him. And to me."

Donovan retreated into a sullen silence. If Veronica had hopes of coercing him into driving her to the hospital again, Laurel expected she would be sorely disappointed.

Upon arriving in Iron Lake, she volunteered to spend a few hours at Veronica's Vittles to place some telephone calls. She was anxious to contact as many of the WRIN volunteers who gave the workshop as she could. Maybe one of them would be able to put a name to the imposter's face.

Besides which, another day on snowshoes might be enough to debilitate her for the foreseeable future. Laurel was feeling muscles she never knew she had.

She wasn't sorry to see Donovan drive off, either.

Tension immediately dissipated and she could draw an easy breath.

"I feel as though I'm getting time off for good behavior," she joked, following Veronica inside.

"I only wish Donny understood the concept of good behavior."

Having the sense to pass on that one, Laurel volunteered to help ready the café for the lunch crowd, since the hour was nearly upon them. Veronica seemed pleased to have her company.

"You're the first woman Donny ever brought to meet me."

Laurel nearly dropped the salt shaker she was refilling. Even as she said, "Uh, our relationship isn't exactly personal," she wondered exactly *what* it was.

"But it could be. He likes you."

There might be a definite animal attraction going on between them...but Donovan *like* her? Laurel figured he considered her a royal pain in his solitary butt and couldn't wait to be rid of her, the way he'd set her aside after kissing her being proof.

"How can you tell?" she asked dryly.

Veronica laughed. "Can I get away with, 'A mother knows these things?'"

Though she figured letting it go was her safest course, Laurel couldn't help asking, "Heard any other good jokes lately?"

The older woman laughed again. "Just for the record," she said, "I like you, too. Anyone who refuses to let my son alone must be good for him."

A point on which Laurel wasn't willing to dwell. She busied herself and was checking tables to make sure they were set up with all the amenities, when the first customer arrived.

Veronica looked around from the grill. "Josh, you're early today."

"And you're late. I was worried, Ronnie," he said, tone more angry than concerned. "Thought maybe you were under the weather this morning, but when I tried calling, you didn't answer."

"I was at the hospital."

"Raymond." He slapped his hat down on the counter and unzipped his jacket. "Should've known. You could have said something last night."

"I guess."

More tension.

Laurel couldn't miss it, not when Josh was acting so possessive and Veronica so defensive.

"So…how's the congressman doing?" Josh asked, not that he sounded as if he were rooting for a speedy recovery.

"He opened his eyes for a few seconds. He'll be his old self in no time."

Josh seemed to digest that for a moment. Laurel passed him to get behind the counter and noted that his face was schooled into a passive expression.

Finally, he bluntly asked, "The doctor tell you he was gonna recover, or what?"

"Well, not exactly," Veronica admitted, "though I'm counting on it."

"Don't get your hopes up, Ronnie. *Anything* can happen in a hospital."

Laurel stared at the man and wondered what he'd meant by the comment. But even if she were willing to stick her nose in their conversation and ask, she lost the opportunity when the outside door opened again, and half a dozen townspeople wandered in.

"I thought I was gonna have to go hungry today!" one of the men complained good-naturedly.

"If I didn't feed you, Aaron Colby, you'd just go find yourself some widow to take my place."

Everyone laughed…except Josh.

"Veronica, what can I do now?" Laurel asked.

"Go make your calls. I can handle things."

More customers wandered in as Laurel pulled a chair over to the wall phone and made herself comfortable. From one pocket of her jacket, she pulled a coin purse. From another, a tablet and pen.

Friends teased her about the stuff she carried in those myriad pockets, one of them suggesting she must have everything she owned in them, including the kitchen sink. At the moment, the jacket felt just about heavy enough, too. When she got home, she'd have to sort through everything and see if she couldn't relieve her load.

She started placing calls, hoping to speak to Jim Evans, the workshop leader who worked for the Department of Natural Resources.

To pass the time while waiting for an answer, she checked out more of the pictures mounted on the wall around the phone. She especially enjoyed several of Donovan taken over the years—from boyhood to manhood—always too serious, always alone.

Didn't he even need friends? she wondered.

Luckily, she found Jim in his office. Her luck held when he remembered her.

"I'm trying to track down someone I met at the workshop," she told him.

"There should have been a list of attendees with addresses and phone numbers in your information packet."

"This particular man wasn't registered with the workshop. He dropped by late Saturday afternoon to visit with one of the volunteers." When she was met with silence at the other end, Laurel said, "Listen, Jim, this isn't a whim. I can't go into my reasons right now, but it's really important I find this guy. I'd appreciate anything you could tell me about him. I don't remember his name," she said, not exactly lying, "but I can describe him."

But the description didn't ring any bells.

Jim was trusting enough, however, to give her the telephone numbers of some of the other WRIN members who'd participated in the workshop. Even so, a few more calls and her frustration mounted. No one was answering. She left detailed recorded messages.

Ready to do the same when she dialed the last number on her list, she was amazed when she finally got an answer. Finally, a real live person.

She went through her spiel again.

Laurel shot up straight in her chair when the woman, Deb, replied, "I think I know who you mean."

Now she was getting somewhere.

"Tall, dark and handsome, small cleft in his chin?"

"Right. That's him."

"Do you know his name or how I can reach him?"

"I don't know anything about him, but Rebecca Kinder might be able to help you. I saw her speak to him."

"Rebecca," Laurel echoed and checked her list.

"Actually," Deb continued, "I think they were disagreeing about something."

"I already left her a message, but if you talk to her, would you tell her this is really important?"

"Will do."

As she hung up, Laurel prayed Rebecca would call back when Veronica was actually in the café and not too busy to get to the phone. She'd ask Donovan's mother to be on the alert.

Once again, staring at the photographs on the wall, she thought about Rebecca Kinder, an attractive young redhead. What connection did she have to the fake Donovan? An old girlfriend? A lover he'd fought with, then decided to make jealous by asking *her* for a drink?

That made a certain amount of sense—a reason he'd know something about wolves and a reason for his being there—but why introduce himself as Donovan Wilde? Could he have pulled the name out of a hat—having heard it from Rebecca or having seen it while reading one of those professional journal articles he'd shown her?—then kept using the name rather than coming clean when he decided to see her again?

But for almost three months?

Now, that *didn't* make sense.

Something else hit Laurel that surprised her...the thought of his being with another woman didn't disturb her as it rightly should. Could her attraction to Donovan have something to do with that?

Gradually, the photograph before her eyes caught her attention. Set in the café, the shot was of Veronica and a young guy with a light growth of beard bussing the tables. She rose and was about to leave when impulse prompted her to take a closer look.

And as she moved in, her eyes widened and her mouth went dry. It couldn't be. She blinked and refocused, but doing so only made her more certain.

It had been there all along, right before her eyes...she might even have seen it the day before....

A photograph of the imposter!

DONOVAN TRUDGED INTO Veronica's Vittles later than he'd meant to. The dinner hour had long passed and his mother's current employees—a dishwasher and waitress who worked evenings and weekends—were already leaving.

Laurel and his mother were the only ones left in the café.

He expected to be given a hard time, if not outright railed at, and so he approached with caution. They sat together, one more grim faced than the other. Gut tightening, he stripped off his gear and prepared himself for bad news about his father.

"Which one of you is going to give it to me?"

Neither said a word. Laurel's hand was white-knuckled as she handed a picture frame across the table.

"That's him."

He glanced down at the photograph taken in this very café. His mother and that guy—Billy something—who used to work for her until recently. "I don't get it."

"That's *him!*" she repeated emphatically.

"Him, who?"

A long look into Laurel's eyes gave Donovan an

answer he didn't like. He shook his head. Her nod practically knocked him into the chair opposite.

"He told me his name was Billy Barker," his mother said. "And that he applied for the job because I reminded him of his mama."

"What else? Where was he from? Around here?"

"Around," his mother echoed. "Drifting. Said he'd lost what was due him and had been having a hard time getting work. That he wanted to start over. Wanted a new life."

"Mine?"

"That's what we've been trying to figure out," Laurel said. "Whether he latched on to your identity out of envy because he learned so much about you from your mother...or if he came here with that purpose in mind."

"Good Lord."

"Nothing good about this, Donny. I'm scared for you."

Thinking Laurel might have told his mother about the trap in his bed, he looked to Laurel and was certain the subtle shake of her head meant she hadn't said anything.

Weird how they could communicate without words at times...not so different than he did with the wolves.

"What now?" his mother asked.

"We find out more about Billy Barker—if that's even his name."

"I have a call in to one of the workshop volunteers, Rebecca Kinder. She's the one he went to see."

Things were starting to fall into place.

"Lost what had been due him..." he mused, re-

peating his mother's words. "That would fit. Mom, have you ever met David Tobin?"

"David...that wouldn't be old Matt Lemley's grandnephew, would it?"

"The same."

"I don't believe I have, at least not since he was a boy. I knew his mother some."

"So you have no idea of how old David is or what he might look like?"

"I'm sure he's only a few years younger than you. And I remember that he was a nice-looking boy. But now?" She shrugged. "*How* does he fit?"

"The land. Karen Tobin threatened to break the will, said she and her son wouldn't be cheated."

His mother's eyes widened. "So David might think he'd lost what was due him."

"If Billy is really David," Laurel said, "then he came to Iron Lake looking for a way to kill the wolf recovery program in this area. With the property reverting back to the estate, he and his mother would be in the money. That would give him a new life, all right."

"Works for me," Donovan agreed, noticing his mother wasn't equally enthusiastic. "What's wrong?"

"It just doesn't sound like Billy, is all. I never got the idea that money motivated him."

"You can't judge a con man by his cover."

She shook her head again. "I felt I had his genuine affection."

"His specialty," Laurel said.

Donovan could imagine how she was feeling.
Lied to. Betrayed.

He could imagine because the same thing had happened to him, the villain in his drama being his own father.

Her obvious pain made him remember....

As if his mother knew what he was thinking, she changed the subject. "I called the hospital a while ago. Raymond responded to another voice. He opened his eyes again."

"With Aileen in his face, I'm not surprised." His sister could be pushy when it suited her.

"Not Aileen. Skelly."

Skelly. His nemesis. The son who could do no wrong.

"Of course." Suddenly he felt as if the room were stifling. "I'm ready to get out of here."

"Without eating?"

"I grabbed something on the way."

At least he'd eaten enough to hold him until he arrived at his mother's place. But any appetite he'd had for her cooking had vanished.

She patted his hand. "I'll pack something for you to bring home."

"And I'll get our things," Laurel said, heading for the back room.

Knowing his mother was set on feeding him, Donovan figured arguing would be a losing battle.

Instead, he asked, "Hey, where's Josh?" The man usually showed before she locked up. "Aren't you seeing him tonight?"

"He had some errand to run, something that wouldn't keep. That's all right. I need to get to sleep early, anyway. I'm going to visit Raymond first thing in the morning. Elvira said she'd open for me and take care of things until I could get back here.''

Elvira was a former employee and friend who'd retired at her new husband's insistence. But husband number three couldn't stop her from getting out when she was needed. His mother could count on Elvira.

And more often than not, she could count on Josh's showing up if for no other reason than to walk her to her door. Donovan couldn't help but wonder about this supposed errand. Did the man really have something to do, or had he made an excuse to save face?

Josh had been sweet on his mother nearly longer than Donovan could remember. His wife had died young, and he'd turned to the Wildes for the family he didn't have but still wanted. Fondness had grown into love, at least on Josh's end, and he'd wanted to remarry and start again. That the object of his affection had steadfastly refused him hadn't stopped the man from choosing to be with her rather than another woman.

He imagined his mother's attention to another man—especially one in a hospital bed—was provoking. Josh probably had no stomach for a one-sided competition.

Donovan shook his head. If his mother weren't careful, she was going to lose the only man who'd ever remained true to her.

"Here you go."

A bulging sack suddenly appeared on the table before him. And Laurel had returned with their outerwear.

His mother started pulling on her jacket. Rising, he helped her into the garment, snaking his arms around her and hugging her in the process. She patted his back in a return of affection. Meeting Laurel's gaze, which had softened on them, he immediately stepped away.

"You two had better get outside before you overheat." He took the keys from his mother's hand. "I'll lock up."

As the women complied, he slipped on his jacket, then hefted the sack from his mother. Despite his mood, he smiled. From the bulk and weight of it, he guessed she'd supplied him and Laurel with enough to eat for days.

By the time he left the café, Laurel was in the Tracker and his mother was standing by the open door talking to her. He'd insist on giving her a ride home, whether or not she wanted it. Ready to lock up, he hesitated when the payphone on the back wall began to ring.

Thinking it was Josh—figuring the man would catch his mother at home—he turned the key.

The click of the lock was punctuated by an angry shout.

"Wilde! Wait up, you bastard!"

Donovan recognized the voice as belonging to Andrew Deterline, the farmer most unhappy with the wolf recovery program. He'd lost both a cow and two of his dogs in the last few months. Not in the mood for a confrontation, he knew he couldn't walk away from this. His gut telling him he had a real problem brewing, he turned to face it.

"What's up, Deterline?"

Coming from the bar opposite, the farmer floundered as he crossed the street, Nate Hopkins in tow.

Neither man seemed in any shape to walk a straight line.

"I lost another animal to wolves last night," Deterline informed him irately. "South pasture."

"Your south pasture directly abuts a deeryard."

Which meant the wolves had easy pickings—deers weakened by a season of hunger. Why would they go for more difficult prey?

"I left the carcass there for you to see for yourself—if anything's left of it, that is."

Another unusual incident...

"I'll be out first thing in the morning," Donovan promised. He'd go now if he thought he could make a determination in the dark. "Don't worry, if you're right, you'll get your reimbursement."

"Of course I'm right, just like last time." Deterline spit, the wad landing inches from Donovan's feet. "I warned you about them wolves of yours."

Gaze narrowing at the crude man, Donovan kept his voice reasonable. "As I've told you before, they're not my wolves. These are wild animals. They belong to themselves."

"Hah! I've seen that power you have over them."

"When?"

Deterline didn't seem inclined to answer. Had the farmer been the one on the property? To spy on him?

Before Donovan could press the issue, Nate added, "Them wolves don't let no one else near 'em."

"Unnatural, that's what it is. What do we need wolves here for, anyhow?" Spittle shot from the drunken farmer's mouth. "Why can't you just ship 'em up to Canada—to the real wilderness? Unnatural," he said again, "mixing wolves with people."

Donovan had heard it all before. The conversation was going nowhere and would continue to degenerate into something ugly if he stuck around.

"If you'll excuse me, boys..."

He started for the truck, where his mother and Laurel silently watched, but Deterline got in his face, alcohol-laden breath making Donovan hold his.

"I'm not warning you again."

He merely stared at the troublemaker.

"Next time I see one of them wolves," the farmer threatened, "I'm gonna shoot it dead."

"You do that and be prepared for the consequences—killing a timber wolf is in direct violation of the Endangered Species Act." At least it was so far. "The state fine can be as high as five thousand dollars, and the feds can get you for one hundred thousand."

"That's only if you catch me." Deterline's teeth bared in a macabre grin. "A man's gotta do what he's gotta do. You don't think a little thing like the law is gonna stop me, do you? I don't let nothing stand in my way when it comes to my rights as a citizen of a free country. Not no one, either—especially not an interloper like you." He punched his finger against Donovan's chest. "You just remember that."

Prepared to defend himself, Donovan clenched his jaw and curled his hands into fists.

But the farmer backed off, laughing. He threw his arm around Nate's shoulders and the drunken men stumbled down the street.

Leaving Donovan watching after them...and wondering exactly how far Andrew Deterline would go in the name of his civil rights....

Chapter Eight

Allowing the engine to lull her, Laurel lay her head back against the seat. She'd overheard those same men in the café, had thought they were crazy about Donovan's controlling the wolves until she'd seen it for herself.

Wishing she could make her mind a blank, she closed her eyes, but other memories surfaced.

Billy...David...*whoever he was*...somehow she couldn't bring herself to hate him.

Didn't it beat all that she still cared, if not as a woman for a man, but as one human being for another?

She'd finally come to realize the difference between simple human caring about a man and being in love with him. After all, thinking about him and Rebecca together hadn't bothered her. Never having been in love before, she'd assumed what she'd felt for the imposter was enough.

But, added to her instincts about the man, perhaps it was that lack of something vital—the very thing she'd felt with Donovan more than once—that had stopped her from saying yes when he'd proposed.

And he *had* been troubled, she remembered.

Because he'd been manipulated into doing something that went against his grain?

She wanted to believe that.

For, even if her imposter turned out to be David Tobin—his goal being to secure the land that his mother thought should be theirs—she couldn't make herself believe he was evil. Misguided, perhaps, and overly loyal to a materialistic mother, but surely not past saving.

If he *were* past saving—truly evil—what would that say about *her?*

Both she and Veronica couldn't be wrong....

Still, the notion made her stop and examine whatever was going on between her and Donovan.

What was to say she would have any better judgment where he was concerned?

Physical attraction was one thing—and she was feeling plenty of that, all right—but she was also feeling something deeper. Scarier. She'd only known the man for a few days, and she already had to rein in her imagination about what might lay between them.

She had never connected with a human being so deeply before.

A few minutes later, when Laurel opened her eyes, they were already driving through the heart of the woods.

Her mind wandering back to Veronica, a woman whose experience with the world and people outshone hers, Laurel asked, "Are you really going to let your mother go to the hospital alone?"

If Veronica thought the congressman was worth fighting over, then Laurel had to think he was, too.

"Tomorrow's a busy day for me."

She stared out into the dark as if it could provide her with answers about why Donovan was being so stubborn. More than once, she'd had glimpses into his unspoken feelings for his estranged parent. She wondered if he knew his own heart.

"We can always find excuses to fill our days," she said softly.

"I don't need excuses."

"No. You don't need excuses. And you don't need people." The fact that that bothered her so much set her on edge. "What is it you do need, Donovan?"

"Peace and quiet!" he growled.

Appalled that his sharp response made her teary eyed, she gave him what he wanted.

UNCOMFORTABLE WITH Laurel's continuing and uncustomary silence, Donovan broke the moment he stepped foot in the cabin behind her. "What's wrong with being self-sufficient?" he demanded.

Laurel shrugged out of her jacket and threw it on a peg. "Nothing. Everything. It depends on how you use it. We only have so much time on this earth." Expression serious—pitying?—she met his gaze directly when she said, "None of us knows how much. Seeing time wasted because of stubbornness makes me angry."

"You're looking at the lowest common denominator," he insisted, shedding his own gear. "Trying to oversimplify. Some things are more complicated than others."

She wouldn't understand. How could she?

"Love can be complicated," she admitted. "You

don't even know how complicated until you lose the person. How long are you going to wait, Donovan?'' She paused, but when he didn't take the opportunity to answer, pressed him. ''Will you wait until your father's gone before admitting you care?''

He could wait as long as Raymond McKenna could. Never once in his life had he felt his father's love.

''He's not going to die. He's going to recover. Ask my mother.''

''This time he's lucky.'' She picked up the sack he'd left on the floor and began unloading the contents into the refrigerator. ''But what about next time, when the *next* killer comes along.''

He turned on her. ''No one's going to try to kill him! He got in the way, is all. He won't again.''

''Some killers a person can't walk away from. Accidents...disease...old age...''

Even knowing that Laurel was speaking from personal loss, he said, ''People recover from all kinds of terrible traumas every day.''

''Some do...others die.'' Her smile was sad as she said, ''And those of us left behind always wonder if there wasn't something else we didn't say or do that we should have.''

''You're talking about survivor guilt.''

''Which has to be even worse when you purposely leave things unsaid,'' she insisted. ''By the way, did you want something to eat or not?''

''If I find my appetite, I know my way to the refrigerator,'' he snapped.

Laurel closed the door and leaned back against it. She stared at him steadily, calmly.

"I would do anything to be in your shoes, Donovan, to have time. Just…more time."

She couldn't hide the catch in her voice.

That got to him, flung him back to the second when he'd recognized his father lying so still on the ground…when he'd momentarily feared he was dead. Then he remembered the way he'd felt so sick inside standing over the old man hooked up to so much equipment. And when his father had opened his eyes for those few seconds, a weight had lifted.

Still…

"There are just some things a person can't forget or forgive."

"Maybe not forget," she agreed. "We can't control our memories. But almost anything can be forgiven. We're human. Mortal. We make mistakes."

Donovan figured Laurel was thinking about herself being sucked in by a con man.

He was proven wrong once again when she said, "I'm not sure how young I was when Mama first developed breast cancer. I only knew she was sick and that my Daddy had started drinking. The sicker she got, the more he drank. Then one day he announced he was leaving before he drank himself into the grave."

Donovan started. "Your father abandoned you?" He left off the "too."

"It had nothing to do with me, he said. He still loved me. And he loved Mama. I didn't believe a word of it, because I'd overheard their arguing. I'd heard him say that he couldn't stand being near her anymore. That she wasn't the beautiful woman he'd married. That she was..." she swallowed hard "...deformed."

The son of a bitch!

Donovan moved closer to Laurel and gazed into clear blue eyes that amazingly held no hatred. How could she forgive such ugliness?

He shook his head in disgust. "Your mother was sick, and he left her to fend for herself."

Laurel raised her chin. "She wasn't by herself. She had *me*."

Donovan couldn't believe how wrong he'd been thinking she couldn't understand his feelings. As for her being part of the all-American family...he hadn't the vaguest notion of how he could have been so wrong making that assumption.

"And you were how old?" he asked.

"I remember the day very clearly because it was my eleventh birthday."

"How did you cope?"

"How could I not?" she asked with amazement. "You make it sound like I had a choice. Mama got better for a while. Then it was the hospital again. I was too young to be left on my own, so I had to move in with Grandma. And so did Mama when she was able."

"Thank God you had someone else."

The expression in her eyes changed to one of pain.

"Grandma was Daddy's mother, and she blamed Mama for chasing him off...for her losing a son. Mama was dying but everything was her fault. I hated that old woman with my whole being. And I was certain she hated Mama even while she helped take care of her. I didn't understand how she could cry when Mama died, not after all the terrible things she'd said about her.''

"People do terrible things to each other," Donovan said. The reason he preferred his own company. "She was angry at her son and she couldn't admit he was the one at fault, so she blamed the handiest person."

Though she remained dry-eyed, Laurel's soul cried out to him. He could clearly hear its voice, still sad if not bitter after all these years.

In that single moment, he connected with her as he'd never connected with another human being...not even with his own mother.

Filled with a surfeit of foreign emotions he didn't want to confront, Donovan said, "You didn't really hate your grandmother, did you?"

She shook her head. "I hated what she did...the horrible things she said...but that's separate from hating the whole person. She did right by Mama and me through it all, and we clung to each other after her death. I understood then that my grandmother had loved my mother, but she hadn't been able to say so. Mama went to her grave not knowing my grandmother thought of her as her own daughter. I vowed then that *I* would never let things I felt for anyone go unsaid."

The way she was looking at him pierced him to his core.

That he longed for Laurel to cling to him now shocked Donovan. He wanted nothing more than to wrap his arms around her and hold her close. To protect her from any more emotional atrocities.

But as he'd schooled himself into doing for eons, once again, Donovan left his heart's voice silent....

A VISIT TO Andrew Deterline's farm was Donovan's first order of business the next morning. While Laurel would have preferred skipping the dead-livestock tour, she didn't think Donovan's going alone would be smart, not after Deterline's not-so-veiled threats. She'd gotten the distinct impression that the farmer would be just as willing to shoot Donovan himself as he would any of the wolves.

Why was Deterline so rabid on the issue?

She decided to ask Donovan about it as they took a back road toward the farm's south pasture.

"Wouldn't you think Deterline would be satisfied at getting fair market value for any livestock lost?"

She knew the Department of Natural Resources paid for animals killed by wolves from donations to the Endangered Resources Fund.

"For one, Andrew Deterline is from the old school. No government intervention to tell a man how he's going to run his place. And then he knows Wisconsin's recovery program has been real successful. The practice of paying farmers for lost livestock could end if the wolves are taken off the endangered list."

Laurel knew public hearings were already scheduled on the matter. If the wolves were upgraded from Endangered to Threatened, monies might be withheld and citizens allowed to shoot any wolves caught taking down livestock.

Even as Deterline had already threatened to do.

Though he might have reason to be angry, Laurel couldn't help disliking the farmer. So, when they arrived at the south pasture gate where he already waited for them, she decided to keep her distance.

The men greeted each other without shaking hands.

Then the farmer led the way to the slaughtered cow. Laurel followed behind and was glad of the gap between them when they came upon the bloody carcass. One quick look was all it took to turn her stomach.

"There she is," the farmer said.

Donovan inspected the tracks around the dead animal. Then he crouched over the carcass and checked it carefully.

Laurel took a few deep breaths of early-morning frosty air to settle her stomach. Thankfully, she hadn't been in the mood for a big breakfast.

Donovan rose and shook his head. "Sorry, Deterline. No go on this one."

"What do you mean, *no go?* You're not going to approve payment?"

"Coyotes have been at this cow, not wolves."

"Bull hockey!"

"Wolves strip a carcass tail to ears," Donovan told him. "Coyotes, ears to tail. Take a look."

"I don't need your fancy explanations. No coyote's got jaws big enough to do that," he said, pointing to the dead cow's throat.

"That is some serious damage," Donovan agreed. "But large dogs have pretty good-size jaws, too."

"My dogs don't do cows!"

"I didn't suggest it was one of *your* dogs. Could be feral. Could be that coyotes took over when the dog had its fill. If a wolf brought that cow down, why would he abandon it?"

"Maybe it wasn't hungry. Maybe it was plain ornery."

"Wolves kill to eat." Donovan turned to go. "C'mon, Laurel, we're through here."

"You'll be sorry!" Deterline yelled after them as they headed back for the truck. "Maybe I won't wait until I lose another animal. Maybe I'll shoot any damned wolf I see!"

Once inside, Laurel softly said, "Not a happy farmer." Not that Donovan's scowl made him look any happier.

"Damn, he's going to cause trouble!"

"If he hasn't already."

A point that Donovan didn't argue.

THE WEATHER HAD finally turned. By the time they got out in the field, the sun had heated the air enough that the trail was turning to slush beneath their snowshoes. And Laurel regretted wearing the borrowed jacket rather than her own. Thinking she might as well be in a sauna, she unzipped it and let it hang open.

Even so, she was too warm even before they reached the first trap, which proved to be untouched.

And when Donovan led her off-trail, struggling with the rugged terrain overheated her.

"Where are we going?"

"I thought you might like to see this," he said mysteriously.

"How much farther?"

He glanced back, his expression surprised at her complaint. "Just over there."

Laurel followed the pointing finger. Her eyes widened, and she rushed to the area he'd indicated. Crouching to get a better look, all she could see was a narrow opening set in the hillside. Still, knowing what he'd brought her to see, she was thrilled.

"Omigod, a real wolf den?"

"No, I'm just pulling your leg."

Unsure now, she gazed up at him suspiciously. "Have you gone and developed a sense of humor on me?"

"Isn't it allowed?"

"Change is good. So, which is true—this *is* a wolf den or you're pulling my leg?"

"If I were pulling your leg…you'd know it."

Laurel took a mental gulp and whipped her face away from him so he wouldn't see the color rise. He spoiled it, though, by hunkering down next to her so close he couldn't miss it. How was she supposed to keep her equilibrium with him close enough to breathe down her neck?

Damn the jacket!

"This is the Iron Lake pack's first den," he said, "used last year."

"Anyone home?"

"Long abandoned. The female moves her pups out when they're six to eight weeks old."

"Won't she come back here this year?"

"She might have to if the weather doesn't keep improving. The pups are due in less than a month. Usually the female starts digging a few weeks before they're born, but as you can tell, the earth's just beginning to cooperate. The ground's still frozen. Alternative sites would be a cave or hollow log. And she might clean out this one, anyway, for emergency use—say if the new den floods during the spring rains."

Laurel rose and stripped off the jacket. "So, how big is the den?"

"Hard to say since I've never been inside. It would be kind of a tight squeeze for me." He stood, his gaze sweeping down her narrow body. "But *you* might be the right size."

She grew even hotter. "I'll pass."

Just her luck—she'd burrow in to satisfy her curiosity and come nose to nose with some wolf seeking shelter. While she did want to see one, that might be a bit too up close and personal for her taste.

"The tunnel could be as long as ten feet," Donovan told her. "And there'll be an enlarged chamber at the other end. That's where the pups would've been born and spent the first weeks of their lives."

"Sounds cozy and safe."

"It hasn't always been that way, though. In the not too distant past, trappers would go into dens to get the pups, either to sell them or collect bounties on their little heads."

The reminder of the dedicated extirpation of the timber wolf throughout the country made Laurel shudder. She'd seen the horrible photographs of proud trappers standing next to innocent animals dead and strung up on a line.

"What would the female do when someone tried stealing her pups? Or the other wolves?"

"They let the humans master them. A wolf might attack if cornered, but it knows when it's trapped and becomes surprisingly submissive. It's almost like they're ashamed of getting themselves into the situation and feel they deserve whatever is coming."

Laurel saw proof of that theory a while later, when she got her second thrill of the day—a wolf caught in one of Donovan's traps.

Still a few yards away, he put an arm out to stay her and stood quietly for a few moments. He shrugged free of the knapsack and let it slide to the ground.

Fear shone from the trapped animal's eyes and bunched its muscles tight. Yet it lay, head down, unmoving, as if it had already given up any thoughts of fight.

"It's one of the juveniles," Donovan murmured. "A male."

"He's scared, poor beast," she whispered in return.

"Everything will be all right, won't it, fella?" Donovan suggested in a soft voice. His movements slow and nonthreatening, he approached the cowed wolf. "Because no one here is going to do anything to harm you."

Awed, not wanting to alarm the animal further, Laurel remained where she was, hands fisting tightly to the jacket she still carried. As he continued to speak to the wolf in low tones, Donovan became a mesmerizing presence. His voice remained soft. Compassionate. His words reassuring. As if he internally understood its fear and its shame.

"Nothing bad's going to happen to you." Donovan hunkered down next to him and held out a relaxed hand. "You're safe with me."

To Laurel's further amazement, the wolf underwent a transformation. The fear left his eyes and his muscles uncoiled. He crawled on his belly several inches toward the proffered hand. When he made a strange sound deep in his throat, Laurel took it to be one of acceptance. Donovan gently stroked the beast's head, and in a repeat of what she'd seen when she'd followed him into the night, the wolf moved forward to lick at the human's lips.

Only then did the wolfman reach into his jacket pocket and withdraw a jab stick, which she knew to hold a mild tranquilizing drug.

"This is going to pinch a little, but it won't hurt you. Honest."

The wolf didn't so much as protest at the careful handling.

And Laurel was reminded of Aileen's story about her cat, whose paw the young Donovan had fixed. His little sister had fallen in love with him then....

And at this very moment, Laurel felt as if she had, as well....

Of course that was crazy. She was merely responding to Donovan's compassion and the fact that he'd sacrificed a "normal" life for the betterment of something beyond himself. Talk about a rescuer—he was the epitome.

She couldn't help but admire that about him.

Shortly after the drug was injected, the wolf's trusting expression began to dim. His head lowered to the ground once more, and his shaggy body gradually went limp.

Donovan thoroughly checked over the wolf. Nodding in satisfaction, he looked back and waved her over to join him.

"You can come as close as you like. He'll be under the influence, so to speak, for about ninety minutes."

Never having been this close to a wolf before—no matter that he wasn't awake—a thrill of alarm mixed with pleasure whirled through her stomach.

At least she assumed the wolf rather than the wolf-man was the cause.

What a perfect specimen.

Up close, she could see that the gray coloring of the animal's pelage actually was produced by white, black, chestnut and gray guard hairs mixed together. Black-tipped hairs adorned his shoulders, and a band of black marched along his spine and through his tail.

"His eyes are still open."

Half-open, actually. Slits she was certain he could still see through. They were a pale yellow-brown, not so different from Donovan's. She looked his way and her stomach did another whirligig as they made contact.

"He's not knocked out all the way," he told her. "Just enough so that I can do what's necessary. If I gave him more, it would take too long for him to pull out and he could get himself into trouble."

He fetched his knapsack and dropped it to the ground next to the animal. From it, he pulled a bundle wrapped in hide that he spread out. Inside were some of his tools.

Then he opened a journal and made some notes, muttering, "Hmm...he needs a name."

"Uh-oh. My grandmother used to say, 'You name an animal and he's yours forever.' Judging by the number of furry critters filling my house, she was right."

Perfectly deadpan, Donovan said, "You have experience, then. *You* name him."

"Me? Does that mean I can take him home?"

He gave her a look that would make a more timid woman quake in her snowshoes. However, having just experienced his gentle side, she couldn't even pretend to be chastened.

"Sorry, wolves don't make good pets," he stated. Then added, "But maybe you can work out some kind of visitation rights."

Laurel snickered. Change *was* good, she decided, wondering how long this lightened mood of his was going to last.

Grinning, she said, "Hopeful." And when he didn't seem to get it, she clarified. "That's the name—Hopeful. You don't like it?"

"Actually, I approve." He scribbled into his journal. "Hopeful it is."

After removing the trap from the wolf's paw, Donovan showed her a distinctive feature.

"He has an extra toe on his left front foot. Makes him easy to track."

First he took blood samples for genetic and disease testing. Then, with her help, he measured and weighed the animal.

"If I weren't already familiar with him, I could figure out his age by pulling a tooth and splitting it open."

Never having been thrilled by the dentist's chair herself, Laurel was just as glad that wouldn't be necessary.

He tagged one of Hopeful's ears with a numbered I.D. "This will help keep track of him in the future, no matter what might happen to the radio collar." Which he then pulled from the knapsack. Fitting it to the wolf's neck, Donovan pointed to the metal tube attached to the webbing and explained, "The device has a battery-powered transmitter that sends out a radio signal. That way, I'll be able to follow his movements using an antenna and receiver.''

"How many of the wolves are collared?'' she asked.

"Statewide, around half.''

"What about the Iron Lake Pack?''

"This guy makes number four of seven. I first collared one of the other juveniles—a sister to him. Then their mother, the alpha female. And a few weeks ago, I trapped and collared the omega, who's new to the pack. That leaves two more juveniles and the alpha male.''

"The alpha male wouldn't be a particularly large black wolf, would it?''

Obviously startled, he asked, "Why? What makes you ask?''

"I saw you together, howling at the moon.'' She could envision the scene in her mind's eye. Another thrilling sight. "Why didn't you take the opportunity to collar the guy?'' she asked.

He didn't seem as if he were going to say.

And before she could push the issue, Hopeful distracted her by trying to raise his head.

"Uh-oh, he's coming to.''

And appearing a little like he'd been on a drunken binge.

Donovan focused his attention on the wolf. "Take it easy, fella.'' Then to Laurel, he said, "I'm going to move him to friendlier territory where he'll feel safer. He'll be confused for a while, but he'll be all right.''

"How can you be so sure?''

"We'll start telemetry tracking him tomorrow.''

Donovan scooped the still-limp body up into his arms. "Could you wait here, maybe gather up everything? I won't be gone long."

"No problem."

Actually, she was relieved by his temporary absence. Give her hormones a rest already. Wishing she could ease her mind, as well, she slipped back into her jacket.

That she'd imagined herself falling in love with the wolfman was shocking.

"I can picture it now," she muttered, carefully folding the gear into the hide. "Me saying, 'I believe I'm falling for you, Trapper Dan.' Then trying to crawl in a hole—a wolf den—when he doubles up with laughter. Of course, laughter would be preferable to other reactions."

Placing the packet in the knapsack, she secured the straps.

"An emotion of the moment, that's all it was. Well, maybe a little more if you count the attraction," she argued. Sighing, she admitted, "Okay a lot more. So, Laurel, what are you going to do about it?"

"And they call me mad."

Laurel whipped around so fast she nearly fell over. Above her stood a woman wizened more by the elements than time. Below a broad-brimmed leather hat, her deeply tanned face was tracked with wrinkles. The stranger was as close to a female counterpart of Trapper Dan as she was likely to see. Dressed in baggy wool pants and a buckskin jacket, a rifle slung under her arm, the woman immediately put Laurel on edge.

"Who are you? What are you doing here?"

"Mad Magda Huber's the moniker." The woman

came closer. "I know yours. Laurel something-or-other." Her *s*'s hissed through the space left by a missing tooth. "I seen you with the wolfman. He's dangerous, that one is."

The weapon Magda carried was what was dangerous. Laurel eyed it warily. "There's no hunting on this land, you know."

"Who said I was hunting?"

"You always carry a rifle?"

"Mostly. A woman's gotta protect herself." Magda whistled, the sound sharp and short. "Course I got *him* to guard me."

The *him* was the biggest, baddest-looking wolf Laurel ever wanted to lay eyes on. He bounded out of nowhere, tongue lolling from between huge jaws. Alarms going off, she took a big step back, but the animal stopped at Magda's side and sat at her heels. She patted him on the neck and chuckled at Laurel's obvious discomfort.

"Good boy, Sam."

The woman had *meant* to scare her, Laurel thought, pulse racing. "You keep a wolf as a pet?"

"Wolf hybrid—that's half wolf, half dog. Not to worry. He don't attack. Except on my command."

Attack...?

Mind spinning, she asked, "You *know* Donovan Wilde?" while hoping he would hurry back.

"The wolfman and me met a coupla times."

And from Magda's expression, Laurel knew those meetings hadn't been congenial.

"He tried running me outta business. Said I was a danger to myself and the community. *He's* the dangerous one," she said again.

"Why do you say he's dangerous?" she asked.

"A person gets a sense of things, living alone, away from civilization…develops instincts…like an animal." Magda narrowed her gaze. "*You'd* do well to develop your own animal instincts, Laurel something-or-other."

Laurel's flesh crawled at what sounded like a threat. Where the hell was Donovan?

Keeping her voice casual, she said, "I'm a city girl. What would I do with animal instincts?"

"Tell friend from foe, for one." Magda seemed to be staring at Laurel's right ear, all the while rubbing her fingers along the rifle barrel. "You need to know when to stand your ground and when to turn tail and run."

Suddenly she hefted the rifle to her shoulder and took aim.

Laurel threw herself out of the way and rolled to the ground even as a bullet whined by her.…

Chapter Nine

"Gotcha!" Mad Magda cried.

But Laurel was unhurt if terrified. Her heart threatened to climb right up into her throat. Then she realized the crazy woman wasn't talking to her.

Walking straight past Laurel, the wolf dog loping alongside her, Magda cackled, "We're havin' ourselves a nice rabbit stew for supper, Sam," and proceeded to collect the small animal she'd just shot.

Swinging her prize over her shoulder, the crazy woman kept on in the same direction without so much as a glance back.

Leaving Laurel limp with relief.

What had motivated Magda's visit? she wondered. To warn her? To frighten her off?

Magda had succeeded at least in scaring Laurel, if not driving her away from Iron Lake. Shooting the rabbit after she'd reminded the woman that hunting was prohibited had been purposeful—a nasty intimidation tactic.

Instinct set her gaze to the woman's tracks. Magda hadn't been wearing snowshoes. Though Laurel was able to discern a few diamond shapes here and there—the same tread Donovan had pointed out to her as belonging to his intruder—the warmth of the late morning had made the trail slushy. She couldn't pick out a single full print.

The *slap-slap* of running feet spun her around again, this time to face an intense-looking Donovan.

"Oh, thank God it's you!"

"I heard a shot." He was looking around wildly. "What the hell is going on?"

"A not-so-friendly warning from Magda Huber." She restrained herself from doing something wild, like throwing herself against him. "Can we get out of here?"

It wasn't hard to imagine she was being watched even now. She'd had the feeling before....

Laurel suddenly realized that Donovan was watching her, his expression weird. Their eyes locked and she was surprised by the depth of emotion she imagined glimpsing in his. For a moment, she thought he might try to comfort her or something.

And then he broke the connection and retrieved the knapsack. His gaze sweeping the area once more, he said, "Let's get going."

As they headed back for his cabin, she told him about Magda's visit in vivid detail.

"I started wondering about this comment she made. She indicated Sam would attack on her command. This may sound pretty crazy, but...what if your father ran into her, and she set Sam on him. His jaws are definitely big enough to maul a man's neck. And she wears the right brand of boots—"

Donovan cut her off. "I should call the sheriff. Have her arrested again."

Again? "It's only a theory," she protested. "Maybe we ought to do a little investigating. See what we can learn about her first."

"Why take chances?"

Donovan hadn't even agreed with her theory, and yet he seemed set on making trouble for the woman.

"What in the world is going on between you two?" she asked. "I had the distinct impression that she's not your biggest fan. Does she have something against you?"

"I tried to stop her from breeding and selling wolf hybrids."

"I didn't know that was against the law."

"It is if she purposely took a wolf from the wild."

"And she did that?" Which would mean she would know how to set a trap, as well.

"I couldn't prove it. She got rid of any evidence."

"Meaning the wolf itself?" Laurel asked. "You don't think she destroyed it?"

"To save herself? She's capable. Even if she didn't—even if nothing illegal was involved in breeding those hybrids—what she's doing is plain wrong and she needs to be stopped. Wolf dogs are a dangerous mix of domesticated and wild animal. They can be unpredictable."

Laurel had heard that before. And yet there were two sides to the story. Even she could see that.

"Magda seemed to have Sam in hand. And at the workshop, I met other people who swore hybrids make great pets."

"It's thinking like that that keeps people like Magda Huber in business!"

Obviously, Donovan's change of mood had only been temporary. "I'm merely suggesting—"

He cut her off. "A few years back, a logger staked his wolf dog outside his trailer. The woman in the next trailer made the mistake of leaving her toddler alone for a few minutes. The kid loved dogs. When he fell, as little kids do, the wolf part of the hybrid saw him as prey."

"Omigod." No wonder Donovan had such a dim view of the practice. "Still, that's an isolated incident. And Mad Magda wasn't responsible for that horrible tragedy, right?"

"What does it matter?" he snapped. "Wrong is wrong!"

Another example of Donovan's black-and-white view of life, Laurel realized. He didn't take the person or the specific circumstances into account before he made a judgment. He'd done that with his father. And then with Magda. To Donovan, something was either right or wrong. He recognized nothing in between.

Making Laurel fear he would settle for nothing less than perfection, no matter the circumstances. Or the relationship. No one could live up to his expectations when he was blind to shades of gray.

DONOVAN HAD EVERY intention of radioing the sheriff's office to have someone pick up Magda Huber. She had no right being on this property armed. She had no right hunting. She had no right scaring him half to death over Laurel's safety.

When he'd heard the gunshot, he'd gone cold inside. But rather than admitting what really had been bothering him, he'd chosen to beat the wolf hybrid controversy to death. Rather than telling Laurel how he'd felt, he'd let off steam in the way he knew best.

Now she didn't seem to be speaking to him again.

He slammed into the cabin to hear a voice issuing an official identification coming through the low static of the radio, which he'd left on.

"Wilde, you there?" the voice went on. "This is Deputy Sheriff Ralf Baedecker."

The sheriff's office had beat him to it.

He grabbed the mike, rattled off his own ID and said, "Wilde here."

"Get over to Nicolet General. Your father's okay," the deputy said. "But your mother asked me to alert you. Looks like someone had plans to kill the congressman early this morning."

"What the hell happened?"

"Your father's nurse was turning him and straightening out his bedding when she found a full syringe under him. No one could explain its being there—and none of the other intensive care patients was missing a shot—so they had the solution analyzed. Turns out the damn thing contained concentrated potassium chloride."

He didn't need to hear more. "Tell my mother I'm on my way!"

Turning off the radio, he noticed Laurel was staring, face ashen. He gave her no time to recover from the shock.

Instead, he spun her around, saying, "Let's go."

No way did he plan to leave her alone with an armed and dangerous Magda Huber on the loose.

Laurel didn't argue, rather raced him to the truck.

Within moments, they were cutting through the forest at high speed.

"Someone trying to kill your father in his hospital bed...couldn't they be mistaken?"

"Baedecker wouldn't have said it if they weren't sure." Though he cursed himself for not getting more details. "A potassium push through an IV port could cause a heart attack, especially if his potassium levels were already high." He knew something about medical procedures himself, though his experience had been restricted to working with vets and sick or injured animals. "Probably no one would question it. A lethal dose of potassium chloride would be easy enough to trace, but only if the evaluation were done right away."

"I can only think of one reason someone would want to try to kill your father. Obviously, he *was* arguing with whomever had control of the animal that attacked him. And if he comes to, he can point a finger at that person."

If...

That he might not—that someone wanted to make certain his father didn't come to—was something Donovan wasn't ready to contemplate.

"I assume you mean Mad Magda," he said. "I don't know. This sounds like a covert plan—pretending to be hospital personnel to blend in. Someone as eccentric as Magda Huber certainly would be easy enough to spot."

"Maybe. If the staff wasn't too busy to pay attention... Wait a minute," she muttered. "The drain!"

"What about it?"

"What if it didn't just get knocked out by someone

working on your father?'' she asked. "What if that was the *first* attempt on his life?''

Donovan swore. If the nurse hadn't caught it, and the pressure buildup had killed his father, his death would have been deemed accidental. And now, had the would-be killer succeeded injecting the potassium into an IV port, his probable death would have looked like any other heart attack—a natural outcome of his circumstances. Two incidents so closely connected couldn't be coincidence.

His thoughts strung out on that grim line all the way to the hospital.

The parking lot was stacked with press, who descended upon them like locusts the moment they alighted from the truck. Grabbing hold of Laurel, Donovan rushed her past the reporters and newscams without so much as hesitating. He felt like a running back, the hospital entrance his goal, as he elbowed directly through the few foolish enough to get in his way.

Inside, government types in dark suits filled one corner of the reception area. His father's staff? They looked to him expectantly as he and Laurel swept by.

"Excuse me. Wait a minute!'' the receptionist called after them. "I'll call security!''

"You do that.'' As if the guards could do anything effective when they couldn't even spot a would-be murderer. "And tell them we'll be in intensive care.''

He didn't stop until they reached the waiting area. There, his mother rushed to him.

"Oh, Donny, how could something like this happen?''

Enfolding her in his arms for a reassuring hug, he said, "That's what I want to know."

Across the room, Aileen sat, looking drained and scared. She was clinging to Skelly's hand. Expressionless, their brother met his gaze.

Guiding his mother to a seat, he asked, "Do the authorities have any kind of lead?"

"Not a clue," Skelly answered for her. "Not that *you* would give a damn if Dad died."

Donovan's jaw worked, clenching so tight it hurt. Skelly always had a way of cutting to the chase and getting under his skin. He moved in on the man who was the pride of Raymond McKenna.

"*I'm* the one who brought him to emergency, or you'd be planning his funeral right now. And Aileen managed to find her way north mere hours after I called. *You're* the one who took his sweet time getting off his butt."

Skelly stood and met him eye to eye. "But I'm here, now, not chasing through the woods with a pack of wolves."

"Not that your being here did *him* any good when someone nearly did him in this morning!"

"Stop it, both of you!" Laurel pushed between them and shoved them apart. "What are you thinking? This isn't about you. Someone just tried to murder your father, for God's sake, and you're more concerned with one-upping each other. You should be ashamed of yourselves!"

"Laurel's right," Aileen said. "You're grown men, but you're acting like little boys. If you can't behave in each other's company, then I suggest you leave." She gazed first at Donovan, then at Skelly. "*Both* of you."

Properly shamed, Donovan couldn't look either woman in the eye. Neither, it seemed, could Skelly, who sank into his chair muttering an expletive under his breath. Backing off, Donovan sat next to his mother, while Laurel took a seat near Aileen.

"All right," Donovan finally said. "What do we know for sure?"

His sister spoke calmly now. "Early this morning, someone slipped into Dad's room armed with a syringe of concentrated potassium chloride...but must have been scared off by a member of the hospital staff before he could use it."

Skelly added, "Baedecker thinks he shoved the syringe under Dad either to hide it, or with the intent of coming back and finishing the job."

"Did he check to see who had reason to be in the room?"

"Yeah. And *I* double-checked," Skelly stated. "Everyone's been questioned. It seems there was a lot of confusion this morning, especially with some members of Dad's staff wandering around, demanding to see him. Too many people in and out. No one seems to remember anything out of the ordinary in Dad's room, though. Just other hospital personnel making rounds."

"No strangers?"

"Every person working here can't know every other person," Aileen said. "Especially with the recent shift changes."

"So Baedecker just gave up?"

Skelly said, "He's working on it. He had an evidence tech lift fingerprints, but the good deputy doubts that'll give them any leads, not when latex gloves are available right in the room.''

"Maybe we should ask him to bring the Tobins in for questioning," his mother suggested, explaining, "I already told them about your theory."

"Problem is," Laurel said, "we now have more than one theory."

She gave them an edited version of her thoughts on Magda and Sam's possible involvement.

"You mean this might be personal?" Skelly asked, voice rising once more. "Not about land or the damn wolves?"

Aileen put a hand on his arm. One look at his sister's face and he immediately simmered down.

"It's something to consider," Donovan agreed stiffly.

Although he hadn't before seriously considered that he might be responsible for what had happened to their father.

"I made sure Dad'll get round-the-clock protection," Skelly informed them. "There's a guard stationed outside his door, and I'm not planning on going anywhere myself, at least not until he's fully awake."

"Has there been any improvement?" Laurel asked.

"He opened his eyes again when I was talking to him a while ago." Veronica sounded hopeful. "He seemed to be trying to focus on me."

And Donovan could only hope that wasn't her imagination at work.

"I want to see him," he suddenly said, hurtling out of his chair.

"Wait." Aileen also rose. "The guard doesn't know you. I'll walk you to his room."

And without waiting for his consent, she joined him. He figured she had something on her mind and probably meant to give him a piece of it. Might as well be now as later.

He waited until the others were out of earshot before asking, "What's up?"

"I thought you ought to know why it took Skelly so long to get here."

"Not interested."

"Stop being so judgmental and listen to me!" She grabbed his arm, startling him into paying attention. "It was his wife, Roz. She's pregnant with triplets. She was pretty upset over the news about Dad, and it looked like she was going into preterm labor. Skelly rushed her to the hospital in time to stop it, at least for now. He came as soon as the doctor assured him Roz and their babies would be all right."

Donovan was thunderstruck. He'd known his brother had married—of course he'd ignored the wedding invitation—but he hadn't had a clue that his wife was pregnant. And to think Skelly had been torn between their father and his unborn children who'd simultaneously been in jeopardy...

He felt like an ass.

What he said was, "I didn't know."

"Because you didn't want to, Donovan." Aileen's watery, red-rimmed eyes accused him. "You've always wanted to think the worst of us."

"Not you. *Never* you."

"We're just people," she continued, lumping herself with their brother and father as if he hadn't distinguished her as being special. "Human beings with human failings. We may not be perfect, but we're not monsters, either, for heaven's sake."

Not giving him the opportunity to argue the point, she rushed over to the guard sitting in front of their father's door. "You can let him in. He's *family*…whether he likes it or not."

"Yes, ma'am."

Then she rushed past him, back the way they'd come.

He reluctantly entered and stopped next to the once-powerful man in the bed. The past few days had been harder on him than he'd wanted to admit even to himself. Should his father die without anything being resolved between them, he would have to live with that for the rest of his life.

Donovan found himself hanging on to a hand he hadn't intentionally held since he was eight years old. And he could hardly get past the lump in his throat.

"Hey, old man…Father…you can't die on me yet. Give us a chance to work it out, would you? For once in your life, try not to disappoint me…and I promise I won't disappoint you. I swear I'll track down whoever did this to you."

His father's eyes slowly opened, and Donovan would swear they focused on him. Just as he would swear he felt a slight but definite pressure from the fingers in his hand. His father blinked twice, as if trying to say he understood, before he drifted off once more.

For a moment, Donovan stared at the parent whose disregard had ripped apart his life. Was there any compromise for them? he wondered. Trying to believe there had to be some way they could learn to get along, he left his father's bedside.

When he reentered the waiting room, however, the women were nowhere in sight.

That left him with Skelly, who looked distinctly uncomfortable. Had Aileen gotten on his case, as well?

"Where'd everyone go?"

His brother stood. "The cafeteria. They're expecting us to join them."

"Wait...about before...I guess the stress was getting to us, right?"

Not exactly the apology he deserved, Donovan knew, but good enough that Skelly did a double take.

His brother nodded. "Yeah, I guess it was."

"Truce?"

"Truce. C'mon," Skelly said, starting for the elevator. "Let's not keep the women waiting. They'll think we've killed each other or something."

"As I remember, we came close a few times. Or you did, anyway."

"I don't know. You might have been younger and smaller, but you were tougher, too. You never gave up, no matter how much you were hurting. You're just like the old man."

"I'm nothing like him."

Skelly got one of those who-are-you-trying-to-kid looks on his face that used to drive Donovan nuts.

Before he could argue the point, the elevator doors slid open. From the corner of his eye, he caught sight of a large red-haired patient, who was trying to sidle by them with his face averted.

Donovan turned for a double take.

He whirled around and yelled, "Gault?" The newspaper man wore a robe over a hospital gown. "What in blazes do you think you're doing?"

Addressing him with obvious reluctance, Ham Gault said, "Don't yell at me like that, Wilde. You'll give me a heart attack for sure."

"You may think you're smart getting yourself up like that, but you're *not* getting in to see my father."

"I'm here on my own behalf." Palm on his chest, Gault rubbed the area over his heart. "I'm a sick man."

"You're sick, all right. But it's your ethics, not your physical being, in question. You're the worst kind of bottom feeder. Skelly, call one of the sheriff's men."

"No problem."

But Gault stepped in front of his brother before he could get away. "Now hold on a minute."

"For what?" Donovan asked. "More of your lies?"

A nurse coming down the corridor asked, "Is there a problem here?"

"You bet," Donovan agreed. "This is Hamilton Gault, the owner and publisher of the *Iron Lake Herald*. He's here for a story, and he's trying to sneak into intensive care to bother our father."

"I'm a patient!" Gault insisted.

Donovan glared at the man whose motives he had every reason to question. "He's lying. And I want him thrown out. *Now*."

"I'm afraid you'll have to wait for the doctor to release him," the nurse said calmly. "Mr. Gault was held overnight for observation."

"Overnight?" Donovan echoed, his mind immediately spinning with questions. "Are you sure?"

The nurse drew herself up. "He came in around midnight, complaining of chest pains." She turned to the newspaperman. "Now, Mr. Gault, you really should get back to your room until Dr. Graves checks you out thoroughly."

"You're right, of course." The big man turned on the helpless act. "Do you think you could accompany me to my room? I'm feeling a little light-headed again."

She immediately clutched his arm. "Slowly now."

And as she led him off, Donovan called after them. "So he didn't actually have a heart attack, right?"

"False alarm," the nurse agreed.

Watching them go through narrowed gaze, Donovan muttered, "False alarm, my—"

"I take it you know this character," Skelly said.

"Better than I'd like to."

"Uh, by the way, I used to be one of those bottom feeders myself."

"Used to be, huh? I thought you still were."

If his brother took offense, he ate it.

On the way down to the cafeteria, Donovan brought him up to speed on Ham Gault's determination to kill the wolf recovery program in the county.

"I can't help wondering if that's the only thing he means to kill," Donovan said as the elevator doors opened. "Is Gault really here to get a story…or did he have some darker deed in mind?"

KILLING A MAN who couldn't help himself should be a hell of a lot easier.

Twice now, others had interfered.

Three strikes and you're out. Or in prison.

A concept that didn't appeal.

There would be a third chance…there had to be…as soon as they let down their guard. But what if that didn't happen before the old man came to?

So many people around now.

Reporters. Cops. Government types.

Getting lost among them was easy. So was getting information.

Every detail of the congressman's welfare was discussed and dissected. Every nuance of his care. Every aspect of his protection.

He *would* have to be somebody important.

Congressman Raymond McKenna. One of the good guys.

How had things come to this? An unplanned incident turned into a nightmare?

If only he would awaken, memory gone for good… Interesting idea. But plausible?

Unfortunately, the congressman wasn't the only one with a memory. *She* had one, as well.

Why hadn't she left?

The leghold trap should've done the trick. Now more drastic measures were called for.

She'd brought it upon herself.

Chapter Ten

The list of suspects was growing.

Laurel wondered if they would ever sort it out.

Skelly had promised to find out what he could about Hamilton Gault's hospital stay—whether or not something was really wrong with the man or if he'd used "heart troubles" as an excuse to get near their father.

How surprised she'd been when the brothers had walked into the cafeteria looking as if they'd never had a disagreement. A temporary cease-fire, she was sure, but better than no accord at all. Even more surprising, Donovan had promised to make it back to the hospital the next day.

At the moment, he was planning to take a shower. She'd already had hers and was wearing his socks and undershirt with a baggy sweater thrown over it to keep the chill away. A shower and something hot and laced with liquor would help them both unwind after a tense day.

The tea was already brewing.

Pacing, trying to find something to do with herself,

Laurel stopped before his workbench. There she spotted the journal he'd taken out of the knapsack earlier.

Curious to see what observations he'd made on the wolves, she turned back the leather cover. The pages flipped open to the middle of the book, revealing a folded sheet of stationary. Not one to read someone's private mail, she was about to page past it when the signature Moira McKenna jumped out at her.

A letter from his grandmother...

She couldn't help herself.

As she heard the shower start, Laurel read the missive.

To my darling Donovan,

I leave you my love and more. Within thirty-three days of your thirty-third birthday—enough time to know what you are about—you will have in your grasp a legacy of which your dreams are made. Dreams are not always tangible things, but more often are born in the heart. Act selflessly in another's behalf, and my legacy will be yours.

Your loving grandmother,

Moira McKenna

P.S. Use any other inheritance from me wisely and only for good, lest you destroy yourself or those you love.

Flesh pebbling along her arms despite the sweater, she slammed the journal shut.

The McKenna Legacy...bandied about at his father's home...something she'd discussed with the congressman himself on the drive here...a prophecy of love that went hand in hand with danger. His family believed in it. And Donovan was next in line. In all the turmoil, she'd forgotten how the idea had spooked her....

Realizing she couldn't hear the shower anymore, Laurel shoved the journal away from her and set it back in place next to several professional periodicals. Wanting a safer distraction, she looked over the publications and recognized one particular copy.

Her imposter had claimed he'd authored an article inside.

Armed with the periodicals, she threw herself into a chair near the stove. One by one she flipped through them, saving the most important for last—the entire issue being devoted to the study of the eastern timber wolf.

Laurel skimmed the contents: "Predators Versus Prey" by William Bancroft; "Endangered Species Bouncing Back" by Rachel Kolnicki; "The Timber Wolf in Wisconsin" by Dick Thiel; and "Alpha to Omega" by Donovan Wilde.

She turned to Donovan's article and was just getting into his observations about pack hierarchy, when the bathroom door opened. Closing the publication, she set it on the coffee table with the others.

The sight of Donovan in worn jeans, a white V-neck T-shirt and bare feet instantly mesmerized her. He lifted his arms to dry his hair, the action showing off his breathtaking musculature. He wasn't even near her, yet her pulse quickened and heat slithered through her.

...dreams are not always tangible things, but more often are born in the heart...

Trying to shove The McKenna Legacy and all its

implications from her mind, she found her voice. "I have the tea if you have the whiskey."

"Will brandy do?"

"Even better."

He flipped the towel onto a chair back and finger-combed his hair away from his face so that it framed his bold, sensual features. Loose, damp black tendrils trailed his neck and spread over his shoulders. Watching in fascination, she caught herself wanting to touch the strands.

The danger part of the legacy was evident...what about love?

She rushed to take care of the tea.

After turning on the radio, filling the room with the familiar low hum, Donovan fetched the bottle, while she half filled the mugs with the fresh brew. He topped them with generous amounts of brandy.

Too aware of the man for her own comfort, she lowered her gaze and clinked her mug to his. "To your father's recovery."

"To his *speedy* recovery."

Laurel's first sip was enough to make her sit up and take notice. She felt as if steam should be escaping through her nose and ears. *Not enough to make her immune to him.* The second hit went a bit easier on her system. The third made her want to slide down on the couch, which she promptly chose to do.

Only Donovan joined her there.

He was staring at her through slitted eyes, making her scramble for a distraction.

His article!

Somehow finding her voice, she asked, "How did

you get interested in studying wolves in the first place?''

''It's a long story.''

''We have all night.''

''Not that long.''

''Then tell it, already.''

He took a slug, as if he had to fortify himself first. ''I was eight. School was out for the holidays, and *he* surprised me by showing up.''

He. His father. Why couldn't Donovan just call him that?

''You mean Christmas?''

He stared intently into his mug as if he were checking out his memories. ''Seemed he meant to take me back to Chicago for the festivities and Mom agreed to it. She was always trying to make me accept him. I didn't want to go, so I ran. I wasn't thinking straight and headed into the woods. I don't know how far I went before exhausting myself. I started getting cold and scared and realized I didn't want to be *that* alone.'' Pausing, he dramatically added, ''And then I heard a wolf howl. The first time is always the most powerful. When I close my eyes, I can still hear that cry, still imagine my hair standing on end.''

Her own pulse was pounding and her scalp tingled, but whether from the story...the brandy...or him... she couldn't say.

''You must have been frightened.''

''Then I saw him. Black and shaggy with glowing yellow eyes.''

''Terrified,'' she amended, thinking of her own re-action to Magda's Sam. And she was an adult.

''Actually, I became very calm,'' he said, meeting

her gaze. "I wasn't alone anymore. 'If you talk to the animals they will talk to you and you will know them....' I accepted him, as he did me. He kept me company through the night. And just before the search party found me at daybreak, he disappeared back into the shadows of the forest."

"Black with glowing yellow eyes," she murmured, her own memory charging. "Could he be a descendent of the wolf I saw you with the other night?"

"Why not the same wolf?"

Now he was pulling her leg. "Oh, please, even I know a wolf doesn't live to be that old."

"You're right. Real wolves don't."

She frowned at him over her mug. "What are you saying? That he's some kind of animal spirit?"

"My Ojibwa ancestors would say so. And probably so would my Irish grandmother, who was said to have the gift," he added, reminding her of the woman's legacy to him.

"But what do *you* believe?"

"I believe in facts," he said, setting down his mug. "That by 1960, the wolf was extirpated in Wisconsin. That it didn't make another appearance until the early seventies, when wolves began migrating from Minnesota into the northwestern part of the state. That I first saw the black wolf before there should have been one this far south. Beyond those facts, I don't know anything for certain, but I leave myself open to possibilities."

Another chill rippled through her. She drained her mug and set it next to the periodicals. "No wolves...but you saw one."

"More than saw. Bonded with him in a way that I

can't explain. Since that night, he's always been part of me. He in me and I in him. I've seen through his eyes. And he's always near in times of trouble...."

He'd been in trouble as a child...and he certainly was now.

Still, Laurel wondered if he could be teasing her. If this was the *changed* Donovan—the one who had found his sense of humor—speaking.

"How much of that brandy have you had?" she asked lightly.

"Go ahead and joke. I can only go by my own experience. You asked why I didn't collar the black wolf. I ask you what good would it do? No one else has ever seen him but me—"

"*And* me."

"—until now," he concluded, voice becoming more seductive. "And I've been trying to figure that out. How you were so privileged. Only one thing came to mind."

"What's that?"

"We must also be connected, you and I."

Was he talking about the legacy? Was that something he could believe in? she wondered.

Or, as in the case of the black wolf, did he leave himself open to possibilities...?

The way he was looking at her annihilated all her resources. Left her helpless. Pliant to his touch.

And, oh, did she long for him to touch her.

He reached out a strong, work-roughened hand to smooth her hair back from her face. Her eyelids fluttered in reaction to his stroking her cheek, her neck, her shoulder. Then he cupped the back of her head and caught her mouth in a slow, sensuous kiss that made the rest of her thrum.

He made love to her mouth the way she was certain he would make love to her body.

Tenderly. Aggressively. Seductively.

Each time she grasped his rhythm, he surprised her, delighted her, overwhelmed her.

She felt herself slipping, giving away control, longing to be dominated.

Caught between a burgeoning desire and what little sense she had left, Laurel fought to keep from losing herself totally in a battle without clear-cut gains.

Pulling away from Donovan, she gasped, "I don't think this is such a good idea," though her fractious body thought otherwise.

His eyes narrowed and pierced her with their intensity. "You don't feel a connection, then?"

She caught a hint of disappointment…and she couldn't lie.

"I feel it." And yet she rose from the couch to put some distance between them, the only way she could regain her bearings. "Maybe too much too soon."

So much more and so much sooner than she had with the imposter. She'd known him nearly two months before she'd entertained thoughts of intimacy…and yet she hadn't known him at all. Besides, she'd never felt this raging passion for him that she did with Donovan. A passion she'd only read about until now. She'd known this man for only a few days…and yet she already felt as if she were a part of him and he of her.

Crazy…how crazy…what was she thinking?

More distance, that's what she needed.

She bent over the table to gather the mugs so she could take them to the sink. Suddenly, Donovan was directly behind her, so that when she straightened, they were touching, her back to his front.

"If something's right, it's right," he murmured into her hair.

Right or wrong…nothing in between.

"How do you know if it's right?" she whispered.

He nuzzled the back of her neck. Heat flushed through her, making her weak-kneed. If he let go, she wouldn't be able to stand on her own. She gripped the mugs more tightly.

"What if you're mistaken?"

"No mistake." He slid both hands over her hips and snugged her to him. "I want you."

She could hardly breathe. She certainly couldn't speak. She definitely could feel how much he wanted her, though, as he moved his hips seductively against her bottom.

"Tell me you want me, too. You know you do, Laurel. I know you do."

He urged her thighs apart with an insistent knee. The pressure…such sweet pressure…she couldn't resist responding, tilting herself against it.

Closing her eyes, Laurel prayed she wouldn't be sorry. "Yes, I do want you."

His hand slid over her collarbone to her neck, then up to her face, where he applied the slightest of pressure along her jaw. She turned her head as urged and, his body still enveloped around hers from behind, he caught her bottom lip with his teeth.

A sigh escaped her and she sought his mouth. He

teased her with his lips and hands, keeping both moving, giving satisfaction with neither.

Smoothing his palms against her bare thighs, he slowly, torturously pushed the T-shirt out of the way. Her fingers flexed and the mugs crashed to the floor. He didn't seem to notice

She was exposed to him. Naked soul, naked body, naked heart. He could do anything to her.

And he did.

He touched…and probed…and teased.

She was fast spinning toward a point of no return, and still Donovan wouldn't let her pivot in his arms. He wouldn't take her. Or take his pleasure of her.

Accepting that, Laurel encouraged him with moans and cries, and boldly slid her hands behind her until she found the placket of his jeans. She unhooked and unzipped them and found hot skin beneath.

His turn to moan.

His reaction shuddering gratification through her.

She freed him from the jeans and stroked his smooth, hot flesh as he did hers. For a moment, his fingers became more intense and less focused. His breathing deepened and became ragged and in sync with hers.

But in the end, he dominated, anointing her with her own slick dampness until she clung to him, forgetting to move, forgetting everything but the sweet sensation that tilted her center to his hand, that took her higher and him deeper until she thought she'd exhausted the pleasure.

But the pleasure had only begun.

The moment his other hand traded her hip for her breast, she cried out. He tightened his fingers around her nipple and rolled it in the same rhythm as he did her more tender flesh.

The quake started deep inside her, perhaps some-where in her belly. It spread quickly... savagely...acutely. It left her limp and satiated, puls-ing and wanting more.

He gave that to her, too.

In one smooth motion, he turned her and lay her on the couch. Then he was atop her...astride her...in her...at one with her at last.

WOLVES INCREASING MENACE headlined the front page of Tuesday's *Herald.*

Finishing a fast breakfast at his mother's café be-fore they headed for the landing strip, Donovan scanned the lead story for any references to his father. They came mostly as a rehashed version of what Gault had already printed in the weekend edition. He'd gathered a few new comments from hospital personnel attesting to the fact that the congressman's neck probably had been savaged by a wolf.

But the main thrust of the article centered around Andrew Deterline's losses, concentrating on the latest livestock kill. No mention of feral dogs or coyotes. Not when Gault had his own agenda.

"If he faked those chest pains to get new infor-mation on your father, at least he didn't succeed."

Glancing up at Laurel, Donovan realized she was reading the paper over his shoulder. A new intimacy. He leaned back so he was touching her more fully.

"Whatever his goals," he told her in a voice low enough for her ears only, "he didn't succeed."

He'd shared with her his worry that Gault might be

the one after his father. The newspaperman certainly
had had the opportunity.

Not that he would be allowed another one, not with
Skelly playing watchdog at the hospital.

And not that Donovan wanted the word spreading
without proof. He already had enough townspeople
angry at him. One couple had confronted him earlier,
before he and Laurel could get inside. And several
sets of hostile eyes in the café watched his every
move. Small-town people were close-knit, and even
though he'd grown up here and his mother was accepted, he was treated like an outsider.

Which normally was just fine with him.

"Did you make your phone call?" he asked.

Laurel made a face. "No answer. Either Rebecca
Kinder's life is so full that she doesn't have time to
return her calls...or she's out of town."

"Or she has reason not to want to."

"Or that." She plunked herself down on the
counter stool next to him. "I feel so useless."

"I have uses for you we haven't even explored
yet."

To his satisfaction, they'd done plenty of exploring
the night before.

Cheeks blooming with color, Laurel ignored his
teasing. "The one piece of information I could get...I
can't get. Damn!"

"Maybe she'll call today."

"Who's that?" Josh asked. Having just come into
the café, he commandeered the stool on Donovan's
left.

"A woman who might be able to identify the bastard who put Donovan's father in the hospital."

"Really." Josh's smile stretched thin. "And how is the congressman?"

"Better," Laurel said. "He's coming out of the coma."

"That so." The older man immediately stiffened but managed to keep his comment on the light side.

Still, Donovan didn't miss the telling sign of jealousy.

Josh ended the conversation by calling, "Hey, Ronnie, honey, can I have a cup of java?"

"Coming up."

And when his mother set the coffee before the man, Donovan couldn't miss her tense expression.

"Thanks, honey. How about we make some plans for this evening?"

"Elvira said she'd come in for me again today after lunch. I thought I'd go to the hospital then. I'm not really sure I can say when I'll be back."

"I see."

But Donovan could tell he didn't see at all.

And when his mother asked what he wanted for breakfast, Josh said, "I won't be staying long enough to eat. Just thought I'd stop by, is all."

"Everyone's so busy," his mother said brightly. "What about you, Donny?"

"I'm going up. Telemetry day." They used a small plane to track the wolves. "First thing is to make certain that wolf I collared yesterday is getting along all right. But I will get to the hospital," he promised. "I just can't say what time."

"Your being there at all is the important thing. Raymond will appreciate it."

"If he even remembers who any of you are," Josh

said, his tone dire. "Loss of memory is to be expected with a head wound."

"We're hoping for the best."

"So am I."

Nervously wiping her hands on her apron, his mother moved away to take care of some new customers. And Donovan couldn't miss the way Josh angrily swigged down his coffee.

"By the way, Donovan, someone's been looking for you."

"Deterline again?"

"Karen Tobin."

The name put him on alert. "She's back in town?"

"At Lemley's old place."

"You saw her this morning?"

"Last evening, actually. She stopped by the store for a bottle of windshield wiper fluid. Asked if you were around or at the hospital."

Interesting. "Any clue as to why she'd want to see me?"

"You'll have to ask her." Josh craned around toward Laurel, saying, "She said to tell you she needs to see you alone." He slid off his stool. "Gotta run."

"Thanks, Josh."

Laurel waited only until the man was out of earshot before asking, "How would she know you might be at the hospital?"

"I was wondering that myself." He lowered his voice. "Kind of adds validity into my theory."

"Do you think *he's* here with her?"

If Donovan didn't catch the tremble in her voice and her strained expression, he might be jealous himself. He wanted to take her in his arms and reassure her. But that would have to wait until they were alone.

"No one's going to hurt you, Laurel." Not while he was around.

While they were expected out at the airstrip shortly, he couldn't pass up this opportunity to probe Karen Tobin's motives. Not that he thought he could make her confess to anything. But his gut had a way of getting him to the truth of things.

"Wait for me here while I see what the widow Tobin wants."

Laurel nodded her agreement, and he ran his knuckles along her cheek. Her eyes got that dreamy look…making him wish they were alone now. He'd never thought a woman could have such an effect on him. And he had certainly never thought that he'd ever find a woman who would accept both him *and* his wolves. He had never felt so connected to another human being, and that both pleased him…and scared him.

"I won't be too long," he promised.

WHILE MATTHEW LEMLEY had chosen to live hand in glove with Mother Nature, he'd never let go of the old Victorian his father had built. One of the finest homes in Iron Lake, the building had been maintained over the past several years as if its owner were expected to walk in the door at any moment. Which, indeed, was now the case.

Karen Tobin answered the door so quickly, Donovan wondered if she hadn't been watching for him.

"Why, Mr. Wilde." Her overly made-up eyes traveled down his person slowly. "How quaint. Come in."

Was she actually batting her false eyelashes at him?

Donovan swept past the woman, who'd made the poor choice of coming to the door wearing a sheer lavender nightgown, topped by an equally sheer matching cover. He held his breath against her strong perfume. He liked his women smelling natural, as Laurel did.

But then he liked everything about Laurel...though *like* was too benign a word to describe what he was feeling about the woman he'd made *his* the night before.

He followed the widow Tobin into a parlor crowded with so many antiques that it made him think of a turn-of-the-century bordello. He doubted this had been old Matt Lemley's doing.

"I was told you wanted to see me."

She displayed herself against a deep red brocade-upholstered sofa. "From the first time we met, I felt we were simpatico."

Donovan merely raised an eyebrow. "Really?" Could have fooled him. She'd been a viper last he remembered.

"A woman knows these things. Sit." She patted the cushion next to her. "Can I get you a drink?"

He took the chair opposite. "I have enough coffee in me now to keep percolating all day."

"I was thinking of something a little stronger."

He narrowed his gaze. Eight in the morning and she was decked out for a midnight rendevous. To impress him?

"I'll pass. What is it you want?"

"I know how fond you must be of your wolves," she began. "I have nothing against them. I mean, I'm not one of those people who wants to see them wiped off the face of the earth or anything. As a matter of fact, I'd like to help them."

"And how would you do that?"

"Every wildlife program needs money. I'm thinking of making a generous contribution to the wolves...and letting *you* administrate it. How does a hundred thousand sound?"

Now they were getting down to basics. Her legal maneuvers had gotten her nowhere, so she was trying a different approach.

"Sounds like a pretty big bribe."

"Bribe? Why, Mr. Wilde, I am shocked you would think such a thing of me. Consider it...moving expenses."

"For me to move the wolves?"

"Exactly."

"And once the wolves are gone, the land goes back to the estate...but wait...not until two years from now. What if another pack should settle in?"

"I trust you'll make certain that won't happen."

"For a mere hundred thou? No bonus?"

"Let's not get greedy, Mr. Wilde. To a man of your means, a hundred thousand will go a long way."

Donovan laughed. "A man of my means. You don't have a clue as to what that might be."

"But you live in that tacky little cabin in the middle of nowhere."

"So did your uncle, and he owned..." he looked around "...this, for one."

"Then what *do* you want, Mr. Wilde?"

"Are you putting yourself on the block, Mrs. Tobin?"

He could see her calculating...

"Are you interested?"

He had nothing against her age—she would be a good-looking woman without all the war paint—but her obviousness was another matter.

"What would your son say?"

Her eyes widened fractionally. "What does David have to do with this?"

She was tense and trying not to show it, Donovan realized.

"It *is* his inheritance, too. I remember your concern over that. So, why isn't he here?"

"He's far too busy with his campaign. He's thrown his hat in the ring for state representative, you know."

"In Sheboygan?"

"That *is* his home."

"Maybe we should call him. Ask his opinion on the matter."

"No! I mean, I don't want to take his focus away from the work he's doing."

Campaigning? Or trying to get rid of Donovan's father?

"Work," he echoed, thinking he needed to alert Skelly. With his media contacts, his brother could get the lowdown on David Tobin and his campaign. And while he was at it, he could arrange to have both mother and son tailed. "I need to get back to my own."

"But you didn't give me your answer."

"You have your answer, Mrs. Tobin." He started for the door, but paused to give her a menacing stare.

"By the way, if anything happens to the wolves…I'll know who to track down. Doesn't take long at all to skin a skunk."

Despite the layers of makeup, Karen Tobin's face was suddenly devoid of color.

Chapter Eleven

Unfortunately, no sign of Hopeful yet.

Thrilled to be part of the chase, Laurel gazed down at the landscape below—mile after mile of snow-covered, rolling land covered with forest in some places, dotted with small stands of trees in others. So far, they'd tracked the movements of the alpha female, the other collared juvenile and the omega. The wolves had been unrecognizable by sight—merely small dark moving specks against a white background—but Donovan had been able to pin them from their transmitter frequencies.

"I think I have something," he suddenly said.

She pressed her forehead against the window but saw nothing moving below.

Smaller animals could be tracked on foot, but because of the wide range of a pack's territory—in present-day Wisconsin, about fifty square miles—a small plane with an antenna attached to each wing was a necessity for research purposes. The pilot flew in circles, starting in the area where Donovan indicated the wolf had last been seen. Wearing earphones attached to a mobile receiver, he switched from one antenna to the other, hoping to pick up beeps transmitted from the wolf's collar.

"Straight," Donovan said.

Laurel knew he was still switching antennas, using the stronger signal to keep the plane on track. Eventually, both signals would be equally loud and they would head straight for Hopeful, pinning him as they had the other three.

This would be one of those events she'd remember for always. In a matter of days, she'd gathered a lifetime of memories. Donovan howling with the black wolf…his work with Hopeful…and most of all, his making love to her.

A lump stuck in her throat at the thought of leaving.

But the congressman was coming out of his coma, and it looked like Donovan and Skelly would get the goods on Karen and David Tobin. Nothing left for her to do—her need to know why David had fooled her into thinking he was Donovan had waned.

Besides, she had a life waiting for her back in Chicago. She had her grandmother's house and her animals and her job.

Only she wouldn't have her wolfman.

Not that she would necessarily have him if she stayed a while longer, Laurel realized. He had something to say about that…and he hadn't said a word.

Want was a powerful thing, but it didn't equate to love.

Laurel believed Donovan wanted her. He'd proven it over and over in the space of several hours. Wanting had taken her through the night. But in the cold light of day, want just wasn't enough for her.

Wondering if he would even miss her when she was gone, Laurel was pulled from her morose thoughts when he said, "This isn't good."

"What?"

"We've got the signal, but it's stationary." He was gazing out the window. "Something's wrong."

Frantically, she tried to spot the young wolf. Nothing. "Maybe Hopeful's just napping."

"I doubt it. He should be hunting for food like the rest of the pack. See that canopy of cedars on the left? That's the deeryard."

"The one near Andrew Deterline's south pasture?"

"The same," Donovan said grimly. "We'd better get down there and check it out."

A lump stuck in her throat as Laurel remembered Deterline's threat to bring down the next wolf he laid eyes on. Not that he would normally see a wolf. But Hopeful had been drugged. Easy pickings.

A sense of doom filling her, she guessed it had as much to do with her time with Donovan running out as it did with the young wolf's fate.

SHE AND DONOVAN went directly from the airstrip to the signal area, or as close as the road would bring them. They set out on foot, minus snowshoes, but for the most part, the going wasn't too difficult. They quickly found a snowmobile path, then another narrower one beaten down by hungry bucks and does on their way to the deeryard.

Armed with the mobile receiver strapped to his waist in an oversize fanny pack, portable antenna in hand, Donovan quickly pinpointed the direction.

"This way."

They were skimming the perimeter of the cedar grove when Laurel started, a flash of movement surprising her. Catching sight of a tan hide, she realized a young deer was darting for cover.

From a wolf?

Instincts alert, she stopped a moment, heart still thumping from the scare. She was getting that weird feeling again, as if something—or someone—were watching. She scanned the area, but no shaggy body popped out of hiding. And Donovan was too focused on his equipment to be aware of anything else.

She rushed to join him, but no sooner did she catch up than he stopped.

"We passed it," he muttered, adjusting the antenna. "Back the way we came."

They hadn't gone far when he stopped again and made a sweep of the area with the antenna, adjusting until he was certain of the correct direction.

"Over there."

But *over there* was a large clearing except for a single fallen tree. Donovan walked right past it. A few steps more and he stopped, cursing.

"What is it?"

Slowly, he turned and followed the antenna straight to the tree stump. He reached into a hollow and, a few seconds later, pulled out the destroyed collar.

"I've read about wolves chewing them off each others' necks," she said, "but hiding them?"

"No wolf did this. Someone's playing games with us."

When he threw the collar to her, she could see it had been sliced open.

"Omigod."

Donovan was inspecting the ground. "No wolf tracks. The collar was taken from Hopeful elsewhere and brought here."

"It had to be Magda, right?"

Who else of their suspects could get so close to a wolf? Not Deterline. Certainly not Ham Gault.

At least...not if Hopeful was still alive.

"Mad Magda could do it," Donovan agreed. "Nothing scares her. At least nothing on four feet. And if Hopeful was still drugged when she got hold of him, he'd be an easy mark."

"Surely she wouldn't hurt him."

Donovan didn't answer her directly. "She could have taken him off somewhere. As soon as we get back to the cabin, I'll radio the sheriff's office and get someone over to her place quick."

He didn't seem in any hurry, however. He kept scanning the ground, every so often stopping for a moment to inspect something.

Saddened, Laurel kept on toward the truck, thinking that maybe her leaving would be a good thing. At least she wouldn't have to stick around and have her heart broken if the young wolf's body were ever found.

Not that she wouldn't be brokenhearted anyway...

A relationship could never work between her and Donovan, Laurel rationalized. Imperfect creature that she was, she was bound to disappoint him sometime. And Donovan had no tolerance for disappointment. He had a history of walking away from it rather than working things out.

Better to separate now rather than after she'd built

her life around him, Laurel told herself. She'd lost too many parts of her life as it was.

Laurel had no idea of how long she'd been lost in her brooding when she realized she'd gotten onto the wrong trail. Rather than paralleling the cedar grove, she suddenly found herself inside it.

The aromatic pines rose fifty feet above her. Thick, clumped branches canopied the forest floor, keeping the snow to a minimum, one of the reasons deer sought its winter sanctuary. Proof of their occupancy, however, lay only in the scattered hoofprints and occasional scat.

The world around Laurel was hushed. Vacant. No visible signs of life.

And yet...the fine hairs at the back of her neck rose.

Instinct like radar, she was absolutely certain she was not alone.

"Donovan?" she called out, the sound of her voice muted by the forest.

No answer.

Hopes that the presence was a friendly one dashed, she slowly turned in a circle, her gaze shooting through the trees and into the distant shadows.

"I know someone is there. Show yourself."

A footfall...but from what direction?

Laurel backed up and tried not to panic when she couldn't immediately identify the passage she'd taken into the cedar grove.

Another sound...closer...one she couldn't identify...made her heart palpitate...

A projectile whistled by her head, followed by a muffled *thw-wun-nkk* from behind!

Whirling around, she saw it. An arrow vibrating from a nearby tree—approximately five feet up the trunk—had missed her by a narrow margin.

"You jerk!" she yelled, praying this was a horrible mistake. "You almost hit a person, not a deer!"

The archer's silence put wings to Laurel's feet.

Blind with pulse-pounding fear, she ran, only hoping her homing instincts would take her straight to Donovan. She couldn't stop to reason out direction.

A second arrow, again narrowly missing her and landing harmlessly in the ground, convinced Laurel that she, rather than some deer, was, indeed, the intended game.

Though her feet thudded almost silently along the needle-strewn forest floor, she imagined she could hear the hunter following. Hear the anticipation with which he took each step. Searching wildly for some escape, she spotted what looked like an old logging road beyond the grove.

Should she risk putting herself in the open?

Or chance outrunning her pursuer until she could find a safe place to hide in the grove?

A no-brainer.

Laurel veered toward the logging road, hopping over stripped cedar branches strewn along the ground. A fallen tree lay directly ahead. Certain she could clear it, she gathered herself up for the jump, only at the last moment glimpsing something weird. And as she launched herself, a third arrow *thwacked* against the trunk.

Attention diverted, Laurel miscalculated and ended up sprawled on her side, her face settling mere inches from dark, unfocused eyes.

Terrified, Laurel cried out and rolled away. Only after she was clear of it did she stop to take a better look at the corpse.

A deer…its throat intact…emaciated…probably dead of starvation…chomped on by predators after the fact. A broken leg…jagged bone sticking through the flesh…a red jellylike substance oozing from the center of the femur.

"Omigod!" she gasped.

A ghastly sight.

Gorge rising, Laurel tried to catch her breath. She scrambled on all fours away from the proof of nature's cruelty. Her first attempt to get to her feet aborted when her legs refused to hold her. Clinging to a branch for support, she tried again. Limbs shaky, she rose and staggered in the general direction of the road.

In the end, her stomach revolted and she had no choice but to stop. Bending forward, she heaved until she was dry. Before she could pull herself together, an arm snaked around her waist from behind.

Yelling, "Let go of me!" she reacted on reflex and struck out with an elbow.

"*Uugh.*" After grunting on contact, her captor said, "Hey, take it easy!"

Freed, she sobbed, "It's you!" and turned to throw herself against Donovan.

His arms whipped around her trembling body even as he demanded, "What the hell happened? I looked around and you were gone. When you didn't answer my call, I figured you headed for the Tracker."

"I did, but managed to get off track." Wishing he

would never let go of her, she was mumbling against his chest. "And then someone came after me."

"They probably heard your scream in the next county. I know it brought *me* running."

Grabbing Laurel by the upper arms, Donovan put her far enough away from him to search her face. She would swear his eyes were glowing dangerously. For a moment, he appeared to be something of a madman, only keeping himself in check by the barest thread of civility.

"You *are* all right?"

Heart thumping, she nodded.

As if something inside him burst, he let out a harsh rasp. "Did you see who was after you?"

"No." Feeling more like herself now, Laurel quickly recapped the terrifying episode for him, ending with, "So, let's get out of here."

"Not without one of those arrows." His narrowed gaze pierced the surrounding forest bit by bit. "Hopefully, your hunter left some fingerprints behind."

"Are you crazy? We could both be killed. Then what good would prints do?"

"Whoever came after you is gone now."

"How would *you* know?"

"Trust me."

Stubborn man that he was, Donovan persisted.

And in the end, Laurel gave way.

She averted her eyes as they skirted the dead deer. He continued steadying her with a strong grip on her arm, only letting go after bridging the trunk of the fallen tree.

Staring at the spot where the arrow had descended, she frowned. "Where is it?"

Gone…

Donovan hunkered down anyway and examined the abutting ground.

"Yep," he muttered.

"What?"

Laurel crouched next to him to see a boot print, two of its diamonds sliced in half.

ON THE WAY to the hospital, they stopped at the sheriff's office, where they spoke to Deputy Baedecker at length. Rather, Laurel let Donovan do most of the talking, filling in only when the officer questioned her directly.

Donovan started from the beginning with the imposter, the trespasser lurking on preserve property and the killings wrongly attributed to the wolves.

Next came his father's near-death experiences—all three of them—and Ham Gault's convenient chest pains.

He spoke of the missing trap and its eventual and unsettling reappearance, to which he added the destroyed collar and the presumably missing wolf, then added Andrew Deterline's threat.

He mentioned Karen Tobin trying to bribe him and their theory that mother and son might have hatched the plot together.

Finally, he related Laurel's scary encounters, first with Mad Magda, and now with the hunter.

All of it.

"Glad you folks have been keepin' me informed."

"It didn't start coming together until a few days ago," Donovan said.

A few days…is that all it had been?

Laurel felt as if she'd known Donovan forever.

"Looks like someone doesn't like you much. Or maybe a rash of someones."

"If you're implying that *all* the incidents are un-related, you're not paying attention."

"I'm attending to you, all right, young fella. Don't get your britches in a hitch. But I'm not making sense of it all, especially not the part about some young buck purposely pretending to be you and romancing Miss Newkirk here."

"That's still a stumbling block for us, too," Donovan admitted.

"*Purposely…*" Laurel echoed. "What if it wasn't?"

"You got me," said the deputy, expression puzzled.

"What if it wasn't purposeful? What if the impos-ter wasn't supposed to be at the workshop…and to cover, latched on to a familiar name?"

And why hadn't that occurred to her before this?

Though Baedecker seemed to be considering the possibility, he didn't seem sold. "And why shouldn't this fella be there?"

"That's the question," she muttered. "Maybe if Rebecca would ever return my call, we could figure it out."

"Who's this Rebecca?"

"Rebecca Kinder, one of the WRIN volunteers. She was seen with the imposter. Arguing with him, actually. I've left her a couple of messages, but so far no go. I think she may be reluctant to talk about him."

"Maybe she'll talk to a man in uniform," the deputy said, jotting down the woman's name and number.

"What about Magda Huber?"

"I'll send a couple of men out to her place. If she's got your wolf, we'll find him. And as for Gault…maybe I'll pay the newspaper man a little visit myself. Never did like him much. Tries to make us look incompetent whenever he can. Time for a little payback. Hmm, I wonder if he's licensed to hunt with a bow and arrow? Something to look into."

"And Deterline and Karen Tobin?"

"A threat and an offered bribe?" Baedecker sighed and shook his head. "Can't see as I can do much without something more concrete."

"We'll try to get that for you, at least on the Tobins," Donovan said, rising. "Right now, we need to get over to the hospital. You'll contact us if you dig up anything, right?"

"I know how to get hold of you." He turned his attention to Laurel. "I take it you'll be staying on with Mr. Wilde a while longer."

Laurel swallowed hard and avoided looking at Donovan. "Well, actually, I was *thinking* of taking the morning bus back to Chicago."

Baedecker nodded. "You do, you let me know where I can reach you."

"Of course."

Tension practically crackled from the wolfman, but he didn't say a word until they were in the truck and back on the road…and then he only had two.

"Tomorrow morning?"

"I was considering it."

"I'll drive you to town in plenty of time."

Laurel felt hollow inside, as if she'd lost part of herself. If she'd thought Donovan would try to stop her, to change her mind, she was sorely disappointed.

He didn't even care enough to object.

"I CONTACTED my old research assistant at the television station and asked for a favor," Skelly said. "She promised to get me what she could by one-thirty."

Donovan nodded. He didn't have to check the wall clock to know it was after one now.

"Don't worry, she's reliable."

"I'll take your word for it."

The hospital administrator had let them use an office that was vacant due to an employee's being on vacation.

Feeling caged by the four walls, wondering where he'd lost control of the situation with Laurel, Donovan paced back and forth.

At the moment, the infuriating woman was waiting for Aileen, who'd wanted to spend some time with their father. As if that made sense. How was she doing anything for his sister by sitting alone in the waiting room? The real reason was obvious. In his mind, Laurel was simply avoiding him.

Skelly broke into his morose thoughts, asking, "So what's eating you?"

At first he considered avoiding the question, but his brother seemed interested and their truce was lasting longer than he'd expected. He wasn't used to having anyone other than his mother to gripe at, and usually he passed on that option. She worried too much as it was.

In the end, he said, "Laurel's taking the morning bus home."

"Better for her, I imagine—it'll get her out of harm's way—but not better for you, is it?"

In answer, Donovan clenched his jaw and slammed a fist against some file cabinets.

"Ah, so that's how it is," Skelly said knowingly. "Congratulations."

Donovan turned on his brother. "On what?"

Laurel's leaving him?

"On fulfilling the positive half of our dear Moira's legacy. 'You have within your grasp the legacy of which your dreams are made.' Don't blow it, bro."

Knowing Skelly had quoted part of Moira's death-bed letter to her grandchildren—not that he would admit it, but Donovan had long ago memorized the missive—he said, "Don't be ridiculous!"

"*I'm* ridiculous? I'm not the one letting *my* woman escape."

"Should I cage her, then, when I wouldn't even so demean an animal?" Donovan growled. "Or maybe I should just leash her!"

Skelly had the audacity to grin at him. "I doubt such drastic measures are necessary. You could try telling her." When Donovan simply glared at him, his brother added, "That you love her, of course."

"Who says I do?"

"Look at you, man—you're a wreck!"

He felt like a wreck. Unsettled. Betrayed. Lonely. Angrier than he'd ever been. And Laurel hadn't even left yet. He hated this loss of self. The feeling that he might have someone else to answer to.

"Even if I did...*care*...Laurel doesn't or she wouldn't be leaving."

"Like she doesn't have a life, right? She's supposed to stay without a reason? Not even an invitation?" Skelly shook his head. "After all the years you've spent studying those wolves of yours, I can't believe you haven't learned anything about *human* behavior. You're still as rigid as you were twenty-five years ago."

"And *you're* still as insulting."

"You're Dad reborn in a different package."

Hands curling into fists, Donovan stopped in front of his brother, who'd perched on the edge of the desk.

"I told you before—I'm nothing like him."

"Hah!" Skelly crossed his arms over his chest. "I saw him in you the first time he dragged you to Chicago for a visit."

"When I was *five?*"

"Old enough to do as you damn well pleased, no matter what anyone thought of you."

"I knew what *you* thought of me."

Skelly gave him a speculative look. "I wonder..."

"You tortured me."

"You asked for it!" Skelly quickly returned, planting his feet on the floor and facing Donovan eye to eye. "You refused to be one of us."

"*You* wouldn't let me."

"*You* always went your own way, no matter what. And Dad always defended you."

Taken aback, Donovan asked, "He what?"

"Defended you. *You'd* start a fight—"

"Because *you* were playing games with my head."

"—but *I*—being the older and bigger brother—was punished."

"Not that *I* ever saw."

"He didn't hit me. No, Dad was more subtle. He waited until you were gone, then would think of some privilege to withhold. I can tell you, that smarted a lot more than a strapping. And all the while, he would hold you up to me as the perfect son."

Skelly was the perfect son…Raymond McKenna's anointed one.

Donovan had known that always.

So what was this nonsense?

Probing, he asked, "He used those exact words?"

"No."

"Aha!"

"He used words like *independent* and *self-sufficient.* You were going to grow up to become a real man's man—while, by implication, I wasn't. He made it clear those were things I could stand to learn. God, the respect he had for you even while you drove him nuts!"

"And all the while, he was telling *me* how creative *you* were. How literate and intelligent. A natural-born storyteller. Said how a man couldn't ask for a more well-spoken child."

"Right. He wanted me to be a politician like him."

"Wrong. He thought you would make a great writer. He compared you to the Irish poets."

"Could have fooled me," Skelly said. "Actually, he did. *Then.* I didn't see another side of him until I got into some hot water—uh, remind me to tell you about how Roz and I got together when we have time to share war stories over a couple of beers. Anyway, when push came to shove, the old man was there for me.''

Just like their father had been there for *him*, Donovan thought…and had almost died in the trying.

''It was then I realized that Dad was a whole lot more complicated than I ever gave him credit for. That, despite our tense, volatile relationship, he really did love me.'' Skelly gave him a long look. ''He could never actually say what he felt. Like it would weaken him, make him less of a man. Don't be like him anymore, Donovan. *Choose* to break the mold. Don't you bury your feelings in pride and let someone you really love walk out of your life.''

Before he could ask his brother what he meant— who their father had let go—an electronic sound got Skelly's attention.

He snapped around to the fax machine. ''Something's coming through.''

And Donovan heard Aileen's voice echoing down the hallway. ''They're here.''

''Just in time.'' Skelly was already collecting the faxed results. ''Bless her heart. I knew that, being a politician, David Tobin couldn't resist a photo op.''

''Good news!'' Aileen announced cheerfully as she danced into the office, Laurel following. ''Dad stayed with me for a couple of minutes this time and actually said my name. He recognized me!''

''I'm so relieved he's on his way to recovery,'' Laurel said.

Skelly grinned. ''Go, Dad!'' he cheered.

While Donovan closed his eyes and gave silent thanks.

''We have good news, too,'' Skelly said, turning a

close-up of a good-looking, dark-haired man toward the others.

"That's him."

Donovan appraised Laurel for her reaction, wondering if her heart belonged to the man who'd taken his name in vain.

Forehead puckering into a puzzled frown, she drew closer to the photograph. "Him, who?"

"David Tobin," Skelly stated.

She sighed. "Never saw this guy before in my life."

Chapter Twelve

"Not Karen and David Tobin," Donovan muttered, pacing the cabin. "Then who? And why?"

Laurel should have known their theory had been too easily formulated. It had made sense. Motive was there. Only it hadn't panned out.

A reason for her to stay longer?

No. She wouldn't look for excuses. Only Donovan could be reason enough, and they'd been acting like polite strangers ever since leaving the hospital.

"Does Mad Magda have a son?" she asked.

"If she does, she's hidden him well all these years. Gault has three daughters. Deterline lost one of his sons and the other has to be over forty."

"Too old. So, now what?"

"You really don't have to worry about it any more since you'll be gone in the morning."

Unless whoever had been stalking her in the woods was determined to do her in.

Because she could identify the imposter? Or did the congressman's attacker seriously think she'd been a witness? Not that she would suggest as much. She didn't want Donovan insisting she stay just so he could protect her.

"If only we knew why he wasn't supposed to be at the workshop, maybe this would all make sense," she said. "Know any wolfmen who are troublemakers?"

"Wolfmen?"

She'd said it without thinking, but...

"It would make sense—he was pretty convincing as you. Maybe Magda or Deterline or Gault figured why not fight fire with fire. So to speak."

Donovan wasn't saying anything, but he looked thoughtful.

Wondering if his mind was on his father's imminent recovery, she said, "I'm glad the congressman is coming along so well."

"He'll be his old self in no time."

"And now you'll finally have the chance to get to know one another."

"I think we know each other well enough."

"Whatever happened between you two was a long time ago. You have another chance."

Surely he could see that. She knew he hadn't gone unaffected by the last few days.

But all he said was, "Right," which made Laurel furious.

"You don't ever give way, do you?" Not to his father. Not to her. He couldn't even express regret that she'd be out of his life for good. Not one tender word... "My God, you're so...so rigid!"

A peculiar expression crossed his features. "That's what Skelly said."

"Then pay attention. We both can't be wrong."

"I can't change who I am."

"No one's asking you to change, Donovan. There's nothing wrong with the person you are. You care about things other than yourself and you try to fix them. You don't wait for some mandate, you take responsibility. Those aren't only outer characteristics. They're inside you, and they're terrific. But you have other things inside that you hide from. Just learn to *say* what's already in your heart!"

"The way you talk about me makes me think you already know what's there."

Was he trying to tell her something without words? Damn it all, this time she wanted to hear them. Glaring at Donovan, she waited. And waited.

But in the end, he turned away, saying, "I need to check on the traps."

So that was it, then.

Reigning in her emotions, she spoke coolly. "This late? The sun's already setting."

"That doesn't mean I can shirk my responsibility to the wolves."

"The wolves. They're more important to you than anything."

More important than his family...

More important than she was...

"They've always been my life."

"Then why don't you take a few clues from them? A pack is a family. Wolves take care of each other and they show each other respect and affection. You play well at being the lone wolf, but you're the one who told me there's really no such thing. That a wolf on his own is merely trying to find his own way, his own territory."

And his own mate with whom he could start a new pack...

Even so challenged, Donovan couldn't seem to break the silence that wrapped itself around his very soul.

Sighing, she said, "Don't keep them waiting."

He hesitated and she thought he might break. Then he turned away from her and started pulling on his Trapper Dan gear. Self-absorbed, he seemed not to notice that she hadn't moved from the spot until he was almost ready.

Then, gruffly, he said, "Get dressed."

"I'm not going anywhere."

His gaze bored into her. "You can't stay here alone."

"I *prefer* being alone."

For a moment, he looked as if he'd like to throttle her...and then he backed off.

Grabbing his knapsack, he said, "Keep the doors locked and the radio on. You hear something suspicious, alert the sheriff's office. I'll be back as soon as I can."

"Don't hurry on my account."

He slammed the door behind him.

Laurel checked the lock and went to a window where she could watch until he disappeared.

If you talk to the animals they will talk to you and you will know them...if you do not talk to them, you will not know them, and what you do not know you will fear...what one fears, one destroys.

Donovan lived by Chief Dan George's philosophy. Animals he knew.

He talked with them…howled with them…trusted them.

Too bad he'd never learned to do the same with people.

DONOVAN PRACTICALLY sprinted all the way to the first trap site. The physical activity helped him work off some steam.

He was angry. Again. Anger—the most familiar emotion in his life, one that both fueled and exhausted him.

Wasn't it time that changed?

That *he* changed?

Laurel insisted no one was asking him to do so…that he should just say what was already in his heart.

First, he'd have to acknowledge to himself whatever feelings he did have. He'd been holding himself in check for so long, fearing disappointment, even that was difficult.

Is this how his father had been? So choked with emotions he hadn't been able to address that it had been easier for him to say nothing?

If so, he *was* like his father. Skelly had been right. Their earlier argument haunted him.

All the time he'd begrudged his older brother being the favored son, Skelly must have felt the same way about him. Without meaning to, Raymond McKenna had pitted his sons against each other, setting them up for a lifetime of resentment and jealousy.

He could see it so clearly now. He *had* been jealous. And why wouldn't he have been? He'd been the outsider. The illegitimate son. The pawn in his father's political career.

Or had he been?

He'd always viewed those trips to Chicago with mixed feelings. Until that time when Skelly had told him the only reason their father paid him any mind at all was because it would look bad if he didn't. Walking away from a child—even a bastard—would be bad publicity. Maybe enough to lose him an election.

And directly after that shared confidence, photographers and reporters had filled the house. Taking pictures of him, asking him questions about how much and what kind of time he spent with his father, they'd driven him to hide in the attic.

And the next time his father had come to Wisconsin to collect him, he'd run away.

All because of what Skelly had told him...

He'd taken as gospel the words of a ten-year-old...one who—he now knew—had been horribly jealous of him. On that, he had based the next twenty-five years of his life.

All on a lie.

There was no excusing his father for abandoning his mother, but that was between the two of them. Either she hadn't held it against him, or she'd found a way to forgive him.

The important thing was, he now realized, that his father had never abandoned *him*. Raymond McKenna simply had been incapable of saying what was in his heart.

And now the son was guilty of repeating the father's mistakes.

Unless he managed to find the words, Donovan knew, *Laurel would walk out of his life forever....*

WITH THE DESCENDING darkness came a case of nerves so intense that Laurel couldn't relax.

Not that Donovan had been gone long. No reason to worry. Yet. No reason to feel so exposed just because the windows had no coverings.

She concentrated on the hum and crackle of the radio, tried using the background noise to clear her mind. To meditate. But she'd hardly begun to relax when Donovan's mother called in.

Laurel flew to the mike. "Veronica, it's Laurel. Donovan's out checking traps."

"You're alone?"

"I'm fine. Is something wrong?"

"You had a call."

Her first thought was of her animals. "My neighbor, Jack?"

"No. That woman. Rebecca Kinder."

"Finally, she called back!"

"The imposter's real name is Will Bancroft. Not so different from Billy Barker, is it?"

"No. Not at all."

Will Bancroft.

Where had she heard that name? Or seen it? Her gaze strayed to the pile of professional journals next to the radio. She grabbed the periodical with Donovan's article and flipped it open to the contents.

Her heart thudded.

He'd told her he had an article in this journal. She, of course, had assumed he'd written the one by Donovan Wilde since that's who he'd claimed to be.

Only half a lie.

He really *was* another wolfman.

Not wanting to freak out Veronica, she kept that fact to herself for the time being, and instead asked, "Did Rebecca say anything more about this man?"

"That he was a sad case. A troubled man whose reputation had been tarnished."

Veronica had told them that "Billy" had said he'd lost "what was due him" and that he'd been having difficulty getting work. He'd claimed he wanted a new life and Donovan had wondered if Billy had wanted his.

"Veronica...exactly how did Billy come to work for you?"

"He was driving through town and had to stop for gas. He claimed he liked the looks of Iron Lake and wanted to give starting over here a try. Josh told him I might still be looking for help."

"Josh..."

The moment the older woman signed out, Laurel looked over William Bancroft's article, "Predator Versus Prey"—detailing moose-wolf encounters in Isle Royale National Park—and found the contents familiar. Donovan had told her about a similar study between wolves and deer that he'd done while in graduate school.

Uneasiness filled her.

Another wolfman...troubled...reputation tarnished.

Why and by whom?

Had Will Bancroft been hired to get the wolves out of the area...or was a personal vendetta dictating his actions?

Fearing she knew the answer, Laurel ran for her jacket. She had to get to Donovan. Had to warn him. He'd be furious with her for coming after him, of course. He'd ordered her not to leave the cabin.

Not that she *wanted* to venture out into the dark...

But instinct told her she dare not wait for his return lest it be too late. Donovan was out there alone. In danger. An unsuspecting target. No clue that he might be up against someone with predatory skills equal to his own.

This rescue attempt had to succeed!

Another person she loved simply couldn't die.

Aawooo...

The hair on Donovan's head ruffed. Having just checked the last trap, he straightened and waited.

Arrrooowww...

The chorus was off...something was wrong. The howls lacked the easy, melodic tones he was used to. There was an urgency to the communication as other wolves joined in, one alerting the next.

Danger...

The wolves were on the alert and so was he.

His internal alarm was jangling...his gut tightening...his spine prickling.

And so he knew...

The alien was again invading his forest, and the night had become ripe with menace. He raised his face to catch the scent on the wind.

Then lifted his voice to complete the chorus.

LAUREL'S CHEST tightened as members of the pack called to one another. Instinctively, she understood they were sending out warnings.

Bancroft was here...somewhere on the property...she'd known it!

Fear burgeoned so that she could hardly swallow by the time she got to the first trap. It was intact and Donovan was long gone. Bending at the waist, hands flattened on her thighs, she tried to catch her breath. To calm herself. To minimize fear so it couldn't control her.

How would she ever catch up to him?

And if she didn't manage it, how would she warn him?

"Okay, Laurel, there's got to be a way. You're a clever girl. All you have to do is use your head."

The wolves resumed their nocturnal chorus, their calls lengthening and growing in intensity. And this time, they were joined by a familiar if distant voice. One she recognized.

"Donovan!"

So far away...

Without first considering her action, she literally used her head—raising her face and cupping her hands around her mouth.

Aiyyyooo...

Fear...warning...desperation.

She tried conveying all in that single howl. Heart pounding, she prayed for a response.

"Please let me know you understand, you rigid jerk. Please!"

Seconds later, her plea was rewarded. The howl was definitely Donovan's.

"Yes!"

Thankfulness filled her.

And then she realized what she had done.

WHAT THE HELL was Laurel doing out in the woods when he'd told her to stay inside?

Thankful he no longer needed snowshoes to get around, Donovan was already loping in her direction, but he estimated a mile separated them. The only way he could accurately hone in on her position was if they kept calling to one other.

Dangerous, perhaps, but necessary.

He kept his howl short and sharp this time. Hers was non-existent.

Why wasn't she answering?

Because she couldn't?

He wouldn't think that way. Nothing bad could happen to her. Not now. Not when he'd finally acknowledged what his heart already knew.

Not when he hadn't taken his chance to tell her how much he loved her.

HIS PRESENCE surrounded her.

He was out there.

The imposter...Billy Barker...Will Bancroft.

She'd beat them all.

Having checked the traps with Donovan twice, Laurel had a pretty good feel for the lay of the land. Luckily, the moon had slid behind a cloud. She might not be able to see him, but neither could he see her.

Silently, an invisible fist squeezing her chest, she raced across the slush for cover and almost reached a thick stand of cedar before a crack split the quiet and a whine winged past her ear.

A bullet.

Omigod!

Hunting her again. This time with a rifle.

But Will's not being able to see her was to her advantage, Laurel decided. She should be able to lose him.

Only she couldn't.

No matter how many twists and turns she took, how many zigs or zags, bullets followed.

He was keeping up with her, must be able to hear her, because he certainly couldn't see her in this dark, not from any distance. Not when she was barely able to see several feet in front of her nose.

Ducking behind the cover of a felled tree, she stopped and cloaked her mouth with her jacket collar to muffle her breathing. She was already exhausted and felt as if she were carrying extra weight. A short rest would do her good.

A minute went by.

Then two.

Just as she was feeling safe, another shot pinged so close to her head, she swore it parted her hair. The only reason Will kept missing was because he was so far away—and that far away, he shouldn't be able to see *or* hear her.

Then how could he know where she was?

How?

Only one explanation came to mind. He must be using a nightscope on his rifle. Which meant that as long as she was in the open, he'd be able to find her.

Carefully backing off, quickly taking stock of her approximate location, Laurel thought and thought…and finally came up with a place to hide where he would never find her.

His KILLING Laurel was inevitable now.

The idea sickened him. The whole murder thing was a concept he'd never considered when he'd started out. He would regret her death the most, but all affected him. He even regretted the livestock, though they had been necessary sacrifices.

Too late to go back and undo anything. His plan had snowballed out of his control.

Why did fate always have to screw things up for him? The story of his life.

His plan hadn't started this way. No one was supposed to get hurt…not physically.

Now he'd have to *kill* four of them, at least.

What choice had they left him? Veronica knew who he was and so did Laurel. He'd been close enough to the cabin window to realize they'd put it together.

As if sensing his escalating distress, his four-footed companion whined.

"Good boy." His hand shook as he bent to pat the muscle-solid side. "Take it easy. It's not your fault. I don't blame you. It'll be over soon."

He would do what he had to.

Self-preservation…every species possessed it.

Making the adjustments necessary to pin Laurel's current location, he went after her.

IT HAD TO BE here somewhere. Laurel was on an incline, searching for the opening in the hillside. The idea might be crazy, but it was all she had. Once she was out of sight, Will wouldn't be able to find her, not even with the aid of a nightscope.

She was ahead of him—he hadn't released a round for a few minutes—but if she didn't find the entrance soon, Will was bound to catch up. Her search becoming frantic, she almost tripped right over it. Stomach quavering, she dropped to her knees in the snowy mush and literally felt the lay of the land.

The opening seemed big enough, but was she really brave enough to go through it?

A little claustrophobic, her stomach doing a nervous dance, she hesitated.

But what choice did she have?

If the passage seemed too narrow, she could always back out. Besides, Donovan had told her about trappers going into dens to get pups—had even indicated she'd fit nicely.

Getting down on her stomach, she poked her head inside. Then her shoulders. With barely enough room to rest her weight on her elbows, she slithered forward on her belly. Her breathing thickened and her stomach felt like a bunch of squirrels were running on a wheel.

Entering the tunnel was psychologically the hardest thing she'd ever done.

Not the hardest, she amended. Burying people she loved was a million times harder. And she'd survived that. Twice. By comparison, facing something that scared her was more in the area of a challenge.

With that bracing thought in mind, she scooted forward, inches at a time, until all of her was inside the tunnel. Now she should be safe if not comfortable. There was no way to relax stretched out on still-frozen ground, cold walls encircling her too close, something hard and lumpy pressing into her hip. What in the world was in her pocket? She tried adjusting but there wasn't room enough where she was.

The denning chamber would at least give her the ability to move around a bit.

Already halfway there, she went the distance. The larger opening didn't give her a whole lot of options, but at least it was a bit more comfortable.

At last Laurel was able to relax a little. She unfolded herself from the cramped position and curled her legs to the side. She even breathed easier.

Until a scrabbling sound told her she was not alone.

She sucked herself back against the wall away from the other occupant. Unable to see a thing in the blackness of the den, she had to know for certain…

Digging her little flashlight out of her pocket, she snapped it on and swept the other side of the chamber.

Fierce yellow eyes glowed back at her.

She was sharing the den with a wolf!

Chapter Thirteen

Heart thundering with fear for Laurel, Donovan listened to the forest, hushed but for his own quickened breath and light tread. No rounds of ammunition fired for several moments now. Even the wolves had grown silent, the strange cracks in the night undoubtedly forcing them to safe havens.

Only wishing safety for the woman he loved, he kept on the same track.

Guided by the sounds of rifle shots, he'd gotten close before they had ceased. He told himself Laurel had lost the intruder. That she remained unharmed.

To believe otherwise would madden him with grief.

Slowing to a momentary stop, he tried to discern anything that would pinpoint direction.

But his *own* senses weren't sharp enough.

Closing his eyes, he silently beckoned to his animal spirit for help, and was rewarded by the hazy impressions gathering in his mind.

Images wavering from side to side…the way a wolf ran, head moving, gaze covering his territory…rugged, rocky terrain…a hillside…a gateway…

Eyes flashing open and ending the shared vision, Donovan raced for Laurel's very life.

"LISTEN, GUY—or girl, pardon me for being sexist— I'm not going to hurt you, okay," Laurel whispered.

The wolf was cowed. Head down, ears flattened, muscles coiled tight, it lay unmoving.

Familiar.

She shone the narrow beam of her flashlight down toward the beast's front paws. One was slightly larger than the other. Due to an extra toe?

"Hopeful? Is that you?"

The wolf gave her a look at once baleful and distrusting.

"It *is* you," she whispered, joyous for something. "Donovan will be so happy to know you're alive and safe."

For now, anyway.

Not that she would share that concern with the already frightened wolf.

"I know you're scared," she continued, the sound of her own voice making her more comfortable sharing the small space with the cornered beast. "But I'll tell you a secret if you promise not to spread it around. So am I."

She'd gone around the bend, making deals with a wolf, but Laurel swore the fear slowly left his eyes and his muscles began to uncoil. She figured, in for a penny, in for a pound.

"We're in this together, you know. If either of us shows our face out there, we might get shot. But we're safe here. We can wait all night if we have to."

Making a whimpering sound, the wolf crawled on

his belly several inches toward her. *If you talk to the animals they will talk to you and you will know them....* Poor guy. She hoped she wasn't steering him wrong.

How would *she* know when it was safe to leave the den?

She reclined on an elbow in his direction to meet him halfway. The lump in her pocket dug into her hip again.

"What is that thing?"

Laurel shifted so she could get at the annoying bulge. Reaching into her pocket, she pulled it free.

"Uh-oh…"

Heart falling, she glanced from it to Hopeful.

No sooner did she whisper, "I hate to tell you this, buddy, but we're in big trouble here," than trouble arrived on their doorstep.

"You might as well come out, Laurel," he called through the tunnel. "I know you're in the den."

Of course she recognized his voice.

As if the wolf felt her rush of fear, Hopeful crawled closer until he was practically touching her. Looking into his trusting eyes, she refused to give Will the satisfaction of an answer. Let him come in here after her. Then it would be two against one.

Her hand curled around the transmitter Will had placed in her jacket pocket, probably at the same time he'd set the trap in the bed. She'd been wearing Donovan's borrowed parka at the time, and her own jacket had been hanging in plain sight.

"Laurel!"

She remained stubbornly silent.

Suddenly, a shaft of light flooded the interior. She pressed into the chamber's wall to make herself small.

"I'll count to three and then I'll start shooting. I have nearly a full box of ammo." He paused a second, then voice ominous, he started counting. *"One..."*

Laurel knew he wasn't bluffing. Chances were she'd be shot and Hopeful along with her.

"Two..."

She might not be able to save herself, but she sure as hell wasn't going to let the bastard shoot *her* wolf.

"Wait! I'm coming."

At least face-to-face, she'd have a chance. Maybe she could talk him out of whatever he had planned.

"Hurry up, then."

"You stay here," she whispered. "Lay low until it's over."

Hopeful softly whistled through his nose, not unlike a dog.

"Thanks."

Laurel shot through the tunnel and out to the hillside, now partially illuminated by the moon struggling to free itself from the clouds. Rising, she faced the business end of a rifle. And her imposter.

"Nice to see you again, *Donovan*," she said tartly, ignoring the pounding of her own heart. She couldn't help herself after so much misplaced concern. "How could you up and disappear on me like you did? Why didn't you call?"

"Cut the chatter. You know who I am."

"Yeah." Slyly, she acted more restless than she might while furtively looking for some escape. "Now

I know you're Will Bancroft...and that you used me. Although I can't for the life of me figure out why."

What she saw sitting a short distance away was a young dog, a rottweiler who gazed up at Will with devotion, guarding a mobile receiver and antenna.

"I wasn't using you, Laurel."

The rifle lowered slightly and so did his guard, she hoped.

"Then why lie about your name?"

"Impulse. I liked you right off. And you seemed to love wolves as much as I did. It was killing me not being able to work with them anymore. That's why I was hanging around the workshop. To feel like I was still part of things. Anyway, I figured you might recognize my real name, especially if Rebecca said anything about my being there, so I gave you the first name that popped into my head."

Not having to pretend shock—that was about the last thing she'd expected to hear—she asked, "Are you telling me I *wasn't* part of your master plan?"

"You just happened." The rifle dropped waist high. "I never wanted to hurt you. I fell in love with you. That's why I asked you to marry me...and why I disappeared. I knew you had doubts without knowing the truth. I couldn't go on with the charade any longer, but I didn't want you turning on me, too. Why couldn't you let it alone, Laurel? Why did you have to drag Raymond McKenna into it and start this whole mess?"

Guilt made her shift uncomfortably, even as he put the blame on her shoulders, when he was the villain. And yet...his voice was rife with pain. She believed he did love her. If so, she might have a chance to stop him from doing any more harm to others…or to himself.

"I was worried about you," she explained. "Afraid something had happened to you."

"But you didn't love me."

"I cared for you, Will. I care what happens to you now."

Even after all she'd been through, Laurel knew that was true. Will might be more troubled than she'd suspected, but he wasn't a monster.

"You're in love with *him,* aren't you?" he suddenly asked. "The *real* Donovan Wilde."

Recognizing jealousy when she heard it, Laurel figured this was one time that honesty *wasn't* the best policy.

"You think I love a rigid, bad-tempered throwback to the last century?" she hedged. "Or that I could get involved with another man so quickly after you? I thought you knew me better than that." And while she was at it, she demanded, "Why do you hate him?"

"He destroyed my life. Because of him, I'm a joke professionally."

Certain she saw a movement over his right shoulder, she asked, "What did he do to you?"

"I was up for a tenure track position at the University of Wisconsin, but I had to publish my current study on wolf-moose encounters fast to impress the committee. I was short on data and didn't have enough time to finish collecting what I needed…"

Someone was behind him. With clouds clearing off the moon, she wasn't kept wondering who. Heart racing, she tried keeping Will distracted.

"So you *borrowed* data from Donovan's study on wolf-deer encounters that he'd done years ago."

"I was desperate to get that position. Wolves are my life. Or they were. This was my big chance to make a difference for them, Laurel. You don't know how hard it's been for me to get as far as I did."

The dog scrambled to his feet, a low growl rumbling from his throat. Certain Will was warned, she held her breath.

He continued, "When my 'Predator Versus Prey' article was published, Wilde recognized the similarities in my data and blew the whistle on me." He whipped around and pointed the rifle directly at Donovan, who was coming up behind him. "*You* destroyed my life."

Laurel couldn't believe the man she loved walked right into the path of the gun. Her heart skipped a beat. What was wrong with him? He'd had the advantage and he'd blown it.

"You destroyed your own life, Bancroft, when you decided to plagiarize me."

"Most of that work was mine! You made everyone think I hadn't done any of it."

"You're still guilty of plagiarism."

Using the rifle, Will waved Donovan over toward Laurel. The rottweiler now sat at alert and watched his master closely. Donovan stopped short, however, leaving several feet between them.

"Why couldn't you have left it alone, Laurel?" Will asked, sounding heartsick. "I even tried scaring you back to Chicago, but you wouldn't go. Then everything got out of hand, just like it always has in my life. The court system. The foster homes. My career.

Losing you. All I wanted was to get even with the man who ruined me. I wanted to make *him* look incompetent.''

"Then why did you hurt my father?" Donovan asked.

"He caught me spying on you. We got into an argument and he tried to hit me. Max here was only protecting me.''

"That the dog you stole from Ham Gault?"

"I didn't steal him. I found him in the woods. He was lost and beat up and hungry. I took care of him is all. And Max thought he was taking care of me that night. I got him off McKenna, but I believed your father was dead, so I beat it. Took his car for a fast getaway. Then, when I read he survived, I knew he'd blame me if he ever came out of the coma. A man with that kind of power…he could arrange anything. My spending years in jail for something I didn't do wasn't fair.''

"So you tried to kill him. And Laurel.''

"You wouldn't leave well enough alone," he insisted, sounding as if he were at his wit's end. "I only meant to stick around and finish what I started. To ruin *you*. But everything goes wrong for me. I couldn't even get this nightscope to work right.…''

Laurel knew Will wasn't a killer at heart. Maybe he'd even missed her on purpose. Like the omega wolf who lived at the edge of the pack, he'd never been able to get himself together to be accepted. Unfortunately, he'd finally gone out of control.

Knowing the man was at a crisis point and could go either way, she said, "You don't have to kill anyone, Will. You'll only make things worse for yourself.

How are you going to get away with murder when you couldn't even get away with stealing some information. You know the authorities will catch up with you. Turn yourself in. Please."

"But I'll go to jail for sure."

"Maybe not for so long," she bluffed, sensing Donovan's intent to make his move. "You need help. I'll tell them that."

"You think I'm crazy."

"I think you're confused." Tightening her grip on the transmitter still in her hand, Laurel tried keeping his attention on her. "I think your bad fortune has driven you to the edge. But you haven't crossed the line yet, Will. You haven't actually killed anyone." Though his trying to silence the congressman wouldn't be overlooked. "I swear if you give yourself up, I'll help you any way I can."

"You'd do that for me?" he asked suspiciously.

Donovan chose that moment to strike. He leaped forward, but Will dodged him. The rifle went off and the rottweiler lunged into the fray, trying to get at Donovan's throat. The wolfman quickly pinned the dog and stared him down, curling his lips and baring his teeth, dominating the animal completely.

Max whined and when Donovan let him loose, slunk off.

Will grabbed Laurel and pulled her in front of him as a shield, his free arm pressed against her throat. She could tell the barrel of the rifle was aimed at Donovan's chest.

Closing her eyes, she prayed for help from somewhere…someone.

"Don't be stupid, Bancroft."

"You shouldn't have done that. Just like you shouldn't have made that complaint against me. You didn't even know me and you ruined me without thinking twice. What would keeping your mouth shut have hurt?"

"What you did was wrong."

No shades of gray, Laurel thought. A crime without a victim escalating to multiple murder…this was beyond her comprehension.

"Will—"

He stopped her by tightening the arm against her throat. "No, Laurel! I won't listen to you anymore!"

She caught a movement from the den entrance. Hopeful lunged out of the tunnel and plowed directly into Will's legs, throwing him off balance. Laurel struck out with her elbow, catching him in the side. Suddenly she was free and Donovan was wresting the rifle from Will. He pitched it far into the tunnel.

Will's rage came pouring out of him in a long war cry. He tackled his nemesis. Moonlight silvered the men as they went flying. They rolled over one another, limbs tangling with limbs. Will was the first to his feet. Donovan rose mere seconds later. Equally matched, they traded punches, but most fell harmless.

Laurel gasped as Will landed a solid hit to Donovan's jaw. His head snapped. He staggered back, obviously at a momentary disadvantage. Will went after him.

Reacting without thinking, Laurel pitched the transmitter at him and struck him in the head. He flinched long enough to give Donovan a break. He readied himself for the next assault. His punch to Will's gut doubled the man over.

Then Donovan flew at him, toppling him to the ground, pinning him there as he had Max, his arm levered against the other man's throat. Grabbing something out of his pocket with his free hand, he quickly jammed it into Will's thigh.

"Aaahh! Damn you, Wilde!"

"What did you do to him?" Laurel asked anxiously.

A few seconds later, Donovan rose. Will tried to follow but couldn't make his body cooperate. Without taking his gaze off the man, Donovan showed her a jabstick like the one he'd used on Hopeful.

"He'll settle down long enough for us to turn him over to the authorities."

Will stopped fighting the drug and fell back. Donovan finally relaxed his guard and took a good look at her.

"You're all right."

More of a satisfied statement than a question. Suddenly stiff and awkward, she nodded. "Thanks to you."

If Laurel expected he might take her in his arms and tell her he loved her, she was disappointed. And yet, the way he was looking at her, his eyes devouring her face, she was certain he had something to say. Whatever it was, she wanted to hear it, but he waited a moment too long.

Rrraa-aaa-woooo...

Shivers slid down Laurel's spine as the young voice called to the night. "Hopeful? He's talking to me!"

Her wolf may have saved both of their lives.

Staring at Donovan, willing him to tell her what

was in his heart, she returned the wolf's call, her thankful, sad song joined by members of the pack...

...the chorus being completed by Donovan, the *real* alpha.

"DAD JUST CAME OUT of the coma," Aileen said the moment Donovan arrived at intensive care with dawn only a breath away. Tears spilled down her cheeks as she approached him. "No amnesia, and he recognized us."

"That's great." Donovan hugged his sister before she could throw herself against him. He was looking at his brother when he said, "And you can both get some sleep in a real bed. We got the guy."

"Thank God," Skelly said.

Aileen pulled back. "What about Laurel? Where is she?"

"Laurel's fine. She was still at the sheriff's office when I left."

"Why?"

"What happened?"

Donovan gave them the short version, leaving out his own heartache. He hadn't missed those disparaging remarks Laurel had made about him. And that she cared about Will Bancroft would have been obvious, even if he hadn't heard her say so. He'd wanted to ask her about her feelings for him, but the words had stuck in his throat.

"So, I came right from the sheriff's office. Do you think I can see him?"

"Absolutely," Skelly said. "Dad's resting, but only because we insisted. He thinks he can get up and walk right out of here."

Straight-faced, Donovan asked, "How can one man be so stubborn?" Then when his siblings looked at him in disbelief, he said, "Lighten up. You'd think you never heard a joke before."

"Not from you we haven't," Aileen murmured. "What's come over you?"

Laurel, his heart answered.

But all he said was, "Just happy we all came out of this alive."

A few minutes later, he stood outside his father's door, trying to work up the nerve to say what he had to. As if sensing his presence, the old man turned his head.

"Donovan?"

Unable to put off the moment any longer, he entered the room.

"Father." The word came stiffly through his lips. It would take some getting used to. "You had us all worried."

"What about you? And that young woman—"

"Everything is fine. Let's save the details for later, when you're stronger."

His father nodded. "I'll look forward to it."

Donovan cleared his throat and began what he had to say. "Skelly insists I'm a lot like you, so this is really hard for me...." He gave his father the opportunity to jump in. When his parent remained silent, his watery eyes filled with emotion, Donovan said, "I'm, uh, sorry I never gave you a real chance before, but I'd like for us to get to know one another if we can."

"I'd like that, too. Son."

"Thank God!"

Donovan turned to see his mother standing in the doorway.

"Veronica?"

"Yes, Raymond, I'm here."

He held out his hand. She crossed the room and took it. Then found Donovan's hand with her other.

"Everything's my fault and I'm so sorry," she said.

"What for?" Donovan asked.

"Keeping you two apart all these years."

"That wasn't your doing."

"It was. I handled everything so badly. Neither one of you knows the whole truth."

"Veronica?"

"Let me tell it while I have the courage, Raymond." She faced her son. "I was a sophomore in college when I met your father. I was very political, wrapped up in rights for Native Americans and in the early effort to get us out of Viet Nam. Your father had recently come from Ireland, a country at war with itself. The situation wasn't much better here at the time. Raymond wanted to change things, but through the system. He was so full of fire. I lost myself in my wild Irish lover until... " She sighed. "He was just getting started in politics and I knew he could make a difference...but not with *me* at his side. My own politics and connections could ruin his career. So I told him I was leaving him and came back to Wisconsin."

"And I was fool enough to let her go," his father said gruffly. "I had no idea—"

"Wait a minute," Donovan protested. "Weren't you pregnant with me?"

"I didn't know until later. I worked up the courage to tell Raymond, only…I waited too long."

"I had already married Aileen's mother on the rebound."

Donovan reeled at the admission. His father hadn't abandoned his mother as he'd always believed. It had been the other way around. And she'd thought she was being noble.

"I cursed Veronica the day she ran from me, but I never stopped loving her. Poor LaVerne. I chose her because she could help me politically. I was trying to protect myself. The first woman I loved—Skelly's mother—died. And the second walked out on me. I never wanted to be vulnerable to love again. But I made a big mistake, one corrected by a divorce that devastated your sister." He held his son's gaze as he said, "Seems I can't stop hurting the people I love."

Which was the closest his father had ever come to saying he loved him, Donovan realized…just as he realized his parents still loved each other.

If his father had only listened to his heart and gone after his mother, maybe everything would have been different for them. And him.

"Listen," he said anxiously, letting go of his mother's hand. "I have to get out of here. I need to take care of something before it's too late."

"Give Laurel our love," Veronica called after him.

Donovan was going to take Skelly's advice. He only hoped he hadn't already blown his chance with the woman he loved.

HUDDLED ON A BENCH against the early morning cold, Laurel waited for the bus that would take her out of

Donovan's life for good.

Maybe it was for the best.

Then why was she so heartsick?

"You know the man has a block of wood between his ears. You could have said, 'Trapper Dan, I love you and if you want to get rid of me, you'll have to tell me you *don't* feel the same about me.'" She couldn't help chuckling at her own cleverness. "Since he'd never express his feelings one way or the other, you wouldn't have to go."

"Don't go."

Laurel's heart stopped. Then began to race.

Suddenly breathless, she muttered, "Great. Now I'm hearing things."

"I thought that's what you wanted…for me to say what's in my heart."

Donovan rounded the bench and sat next to her, but Laurel was afraid to look at him.

"Don't go," he said again.

"But I have a whole life in—"

"Change it."

Demanding, as usual.

"And animals. *Lots* of animals," she warned him.

"Plenty of room for them up here."

She sighed. "And medical debts—"

"We'll take care of them."

"We?" Finally, Laurel tilted her face toward Donovan. Her heart pounding furiously, she asked, "What are you trying to say?"

Donovan's expression was so serious, her heart wrenched. He was having enough trouble beating around the bush. Maybe it was enough that he asked her not to go.

Taking her hand, he said, "I've never met a woman like you before."

"Like what?"

"One who talks to animals."

"That's it?"

"And who has the guts to crawl into a wolf den."

"How did you know?"

"I talk to animals, remember. We'd make some team, working side by side."

"You want to give me a job as a tracker?" she asked, only half joking. Why couldn't he just *say* it? "I have no real training."

"I could teach you."

A roar up the street caught her attention. The bus to Chicago was just down the block. And Laurel decided Donovan's not wanting her to go *wasn't* enough. She stood and looked away, concentrated on the approaching bus.

"Laurel?"

"Uh-huh?"

She refused to look at him lest he see the tears in her eyes.

"Actually...that working side-by-side thing...I had something else in mind...I was considering starting a pack of my own."

The bus was slowing.

"If you're trying to tell me you love me, you'd better—"

Taking her in his arms, he shouted, "I love you!"

Her eyes widened. "Omigod, you said it."

"So, what do *you* say? Will you stay?"

Waving the bus on, she threw her arms around his neck and laughed through tears of happiness.

Then she lifted her face and howled.

Epilogue

For the first time in his life, Donovan entered his father's home without reservations.

Everything was different.

Not the house itself or its furnishings.

He was different.

And with Laurel at his side, he could face anything.

"Donovan, you took long enough getting here from the church," Aileen said. "I thought you weren't coming."

"It's the parking," Laurel grumbled. "I thought we were going to have to walk a mile...and then someone cleared out right in front."

"Laurel, I need your help."

Before Donovan could protest, his sister dragged her off.

Standing at the liquor cart with Tyler Leighton, Skelly waved him over. "How about a drink? We were just getting set to toast Miss Kelly McKenna Leighton."

"I'll drink to that. Whatever you're having."

It was in honor of the newest addition that the family had gathered together. A christening. A time to celebrate.

Holding Kelly, Keelin smiled at him. "Gran would be well satisfied with herself if she saw you with your Laurel."

"The McKenna Legacy at work. I was helpless to resist."

He and Laurel would wed the following month.

And Donovan wondered about his father and mother being next in line. They hadn't made any commitments yet, but from the way they were looking at one another, he suspected that would come.

His brother handed him his drink. "Here you go, bro."

"Thanks. And, Skelly, I've been meaning to say something to you."

"Uh-oh. That the truce is over?"

"That I forgive you."

"For what?"

Donovan doubted that his brother even remembered the lie. "For whatever transgression you need forgiveness for."

Skelly laughed and yelled, "Laurel, you're a marvel!"

From the couch, Roz gave a yelp. "My water just broke!"

From the looks of her, Donovan was surprised she hadn't delivered long ago.

"You're in labor?" Skelly rushed to her side. "Why didn't you say something?"

"I didn't want to spoil the day for anyone."

"Don't be standing around and gawking now,"

Keelin said. "Let's get the poor woman to the hospital."

"Ooohhh, I hope I make it."

"They're coming? Anyone know what to do if we don't make it in time?"

Amused at his brother's panic, Donovan volunteered, "I've had some experience assisting births...of wolves."

"Leave the poor man alone," Laurel whispered.

He drew her to him and kissed her.

Everyone was rushing around...getting coats... helping Roz to the door.

"Donovan, what are you waiting for?" Aileen demanded of him. "You're parked right out front. Aren't you going to drive them?"

"You want *me* to go to the hospital?"

"Are you part of this family or not?"

"Absolutely."

He grabbed Laurel's hand and rushed to the door.

For the first time in his life, Donovan felt like a McKenna.

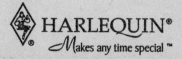

Catch more great

HARLEQUIN™ Movies

featured on **the movie channel** (tmc)

Premiering September 12th
A Change of Place
Starring Rick Springfield and
Stephanie Beacham. Based on the novel
by bestselling author Tracy Sinclair

Don't miss next month's movie!
Premiering October 10th
Loving Evangeline
Based on the novel by *New York Times*
bestselling author Linda Howard

If you are not currently a subscriber to
The Movie Channel, simply call your
local cable or satellite provider for more
details. Call today, and don't miss out
on the romance!

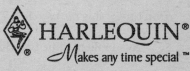

the movie channel (tmc)   **HARLEQUIN**®

100% pure movies.   *Makes any time special* ™
100% pure fun.

Lost & Found

All new...and filled with the mystery and romance you love!

SOMEBODY'S BABY
by Amanda Stevens in November 1998

A FATHER FOR HER BABY
by B. J. Daniels in December 1998

A FATHER'S LOVE
by Carla Cassidy in January 1999

It all begins one night when three women go into labor in the same Galveston, Texas, hospital. Shortly after the babies are born, fire erupts, and though each child and mother make it to safety, there's more than just the mystery of birth to solve now....

Don't miss this *all new* LOST & FOUND trilogy!

Available at your favorite retail outlet.

HARLEQUIN®
Makes any time special ™

MEN at WORK

All work and no play?
Not these men!

July 1998

MACKENZIE'S LADY by Dallas Schulze

Undercover agent Mackenzie Donahue's
lazy smile and deep blue eyes were his best
weapons. But after rescuing—and kissing!—
damsel in distress Holly Reynolds, how could
he betray her by spying on her brother?

August 1998

MISS LIZ'S PASSION by Sherryl Woods

Todd Lewis could put up a building with ease,
but quailed at the sight of a classroom! Still,
Liz Gentry, his son's teacher, was no battle-ax,
and soon Todd started planning some
extracurricular activities of his own....

September 1998

A CLASSIC ENCOUNTER
by Emilie Richards

Doctor Chris Matthews was intelligent, sexy
and *very* good with his hands—which made
him all the more dangerous to single mom
Lizette St. Hilaire. So how long could she
resist Chris's special brand of TLC?

Available at your favorite retail outlet!

MEN AT WORK™

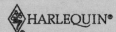 

COMING NEXT MONTH

#485 REMEMBER ME, COWBOY by Caroline Burnes
Cassidy O'Neal's world shattered the day Slate Walker lost his
memory and was convicted of a crime she was sure he hadn't
committed. Five years later, she'd risk her ranch and her heart to
prove him innocent…but could she tell him about the daughter he
never knew they had?

#486 SEND ME A HERO by Rita Herron
Her Protector
Echoing footsteps, threatening phone calls, a midnight attacker…
Veronica Miller knew she was in danger, but police could find no
evidence. Someone wanted her to look crazy. Could Detective
Nathan Dawson save Veronica from events set in motion far in the
past, on a night she couldn't remember?

#487 MYSTERY DAD by Leona Karr
Mark Richards was stunned when he came home to find his bachelor
apartment occupied by two youngsters and a baby. Working with P.I.
Kerri Kincaid to find the missing mother placed both Mark and Kerri
in danger—and the biggest threat was to Mark's bachelor status.…

#488 THE ARMS OF THE LAW by Jenna Ryan
Psychiatrist Nikita Sorensen was shaken by the hospital murders—
and unsettled by officer Daniel Vachon whose bold approach to the
case squared him head-to-head with Nikita. But it was soon clear the
murderer aimed to draw Nikita into the web of terror. And Vachon's
strong arms were the only safe harbor.

AVAILABLE THIS MONTH:

Look us up on-line at: http://www.romance.net